> To Steve & Maryone How
> Thank you &
> for your support.
> been a great inspiration
> me spit out my coffee several
> from laughing at your jokes, esp
> on the morning show! I appreciate you
> both. Smooches :)
> T. M.

OPEN MARRIAGE

(A NOVEL)

OPEN MARRIAGE

(A NOVEL)

TIFFANY MCGEE

TMG Book Publishing
Miramar, Florida

OPEN MARRIAGE

Published by:

TMG Book Publishing
Miramar, Florida
Tiff.mcgee94@gmail.com

Tiffany McGee, Publisher
Enviro Creative. Cover Designer
Quality Press.info, Book Packager

ALL RIGHTS RESERVED

No parts of this book may be reproduced or transmitted in any form or by any means electronic or mechanical, including photocopying, recording or any information storage and retrieved system without the written permission from the authors, except for the inclusion of brief quotations in review.

The publication is sold with the understanding that the Publisher is not engaged in rendering legal or other professional services. If legal advice or other expert assistance is required, the services of a competent professional person should be sought.

DISCLAIMER: The characters in this book are fictitious. Any similarity to real persons, living or dead, is coincidental and not intended by the author.

Copyright © 2022 by Tiffany McGee
Paperback ISBN #: 979-8-9858627-0-6
Ebook ISBN #: 979-8-9858627-1-3
Library of Congress Control Number: 2022904373

DEDICATION

This book is dedicated to the most important people in my life after God. They are my daughter Tianna and my mother Kathy. The two of them combined have provided the inspiration and encouragement to continue becoming so that I can *Become*.

Tiffany McGee

ACKNOWLEDGEMENTS

First and foremost, I would like to thank my God for the courage to publish.

I would like to send a special thanks to my mother, Kathy Davis, and my family that helped provide the life for me where I have my own stories and have had the opportunity to meet others with their stories as well. Thank you to my daughter who has been an inspiration.

I would like to thank everyone that played a part in providing their experiences to this book. I want to thank all of the people that I met over the years who have shared their stories of their adventures.

I would also like to thank the people that encouraged me to put this information in writing so that these stories can be heard. I appreciate the encouragement from family, friends and acquaintances to publish this book.

If it is God's will, there will be more to come.

Tiffany McGee

CONTENTS

Dedication v

Acknowledgements vii

Prologue xi

Chapter One 1

Chapter Two 7

Chapter Three 13

Chapter Four 23

Chapter Five 52

Chapter Six 86

Chapter Seven 128

About the Author 161

Tiffany McGee

PROLOGUE

It's a Saturday night. The bath was warm the bubbles were soft, and he was feeling good. We were kissing and making out. I straddled him as I faced him, and we continued to kiss. After a while of kissing and biting, he stopped me and said, "I was told that you had a crush on me. Is that true?" Shortly after, I replied with a great big smile and a yes. We continued to kiss and make out while we were together in the bubble bath. I was overjoyed because I really had liked him for a while. We had been friends for five years prior to this evening. I knew him when he was the vice president of the Black Student Union at our school and very active on campus; he inspired me when we met. I thought that he was very smart and articulate and that he was the type of man that I would aspire to marry sometime down the road.

Tiffany McGee

CHAPTER ONE

Now we are together in a manner that I hadn't expected; but nonetheless, he met the standards that I had at the time. He had some ambition and he knew God. He also was attractive, and we had very deep discussions on several different topics… so he seemed well-rounded. Back to the tub, we began making out some more while I still had him straddled and he stopped me again. He asked me a question. "Will this be enough for you?" he said, while looking down and holding his manhood. "Will you be satisfied with this?" I looked at him and smiled, "of course, what's wrong with what you have?" He said, "I just want to make sure that you will be satisfied with what I have to offer." My response was, "If I didn't think you could satisfy me, we wouldn't be here right now together, connecting our souls as we are. I have no problems with what you are carrying. You should have more confidence, baby. I really like you. I have since we met when I was a freshman, but I never acted on it because we were friends and I value our friendship. Now that I have graduated and school is behind us, we can see how you and I work out."

He grabbed me tighter and we began kissing more. I thought this was the beginning of a wonderful relationship and I was so engulfed in the feelings that overcame my body as we kissed and held each other. After some more making out, he stopped us again. He said, "I think we should keep open boundaries if we are going to be in a relationship. I don't want us to break up because of cheating or something like that. I think that we should be able to work through whatever problems may arise with us if that ever happens."

I smiled and said simply, "ok." I was really into him and he could have said anything, and I would have agreed. "Please keep in mind that while all of this is going on we have wine, weed, and ecstasy." We liked rolling on ecstasy because it made everything feel good. Of course, ecstasy is a drug and it affects your thinking as well. Taking ecstasy to relax and make us more "touchy feely" was something that turned us both on even more. Just so that this evening is in perspective, we were high, but in our right mind as the night had just started. Ecstasy allowed us to let go of our inhibitions and really let loose with each other. Sitting in the tub with warm bubbles was something that I liked to do because it felt so good when I was rolling on ecstasy. He joined me in the tub because we were already quite smitten with each other and neither had said anything about it, but as you can see, we spoke on those feelings this evening. More making out, kissing, biting, licking and everything that made the two of us feel good was what continued to happen in the tub that night, along with establishing that we would now be in an official relationship. I won't call it exclusive because he had already spelled out the boundaries or lack thereof of this relationship that we were about to embark on.

That night was great. We became official lovers and we had the same hobbies and habits so that worked for me as I didn't have to be secretive or keep anything from him. I could truly be myself. I let down my wall and my guard and he became my man and I was his lady. After that, our weekends consisted of rolling on ecstasy and making love. Of course, there were other events. We went to parties and clubs. We had a male friend that was gay, and he took us to the gay club a lot. There would be a lot of people at these clubs rolling on ecstasy as well, and we fit right in. we just wanted to party, dance and drink until the night ended. Usually, once the night ended, my man and I would go and make love. I mean rough passionate sex until we absolutely couldn't move anymore. That was how our relationship started and I really felt like life was great. I was in my early 20s and had no other responsibilities besides the usual like someplace to live; lights, phone and car insurance. I had an older car, so thank goodness I didn't have a car note at the time.

One night we were hanging out with some different friends. We were smoking, drinking, and rolling like we did to unwind. It's not like we were drug addicts or anything. We both worked 40-hour-a-week jobs and made sure we had our rest and replenishment before the week began; so that when it was time for work on Monday morning, we were recuperated, relaxed, and ready for the week. We went to work Monday through Friday. We didn't party too much during the week. We just had a drink or two after work some days and a joint most times. The weed or marijuana as it is usually called was what we did daily. I can't say what it does for them, but for me it helps me to calm down and relax because my brain is always on overload. I can't stop the thoughts and sometimes I want the noise and brain chatter to stop so that I can take a break from it. Back to this particular night, my man and I were chilling out with some friends. We would go over there every so often, so we all knew each other for some time. While hanging out this night, one of the people there that would lightly flirt with me asked me to take it further with him. This guy was named Josh. Josh was a nice-looking white boy from Louisiana.. Word had gotten out that my guy and I had an open relationship; therefore, Josh approached me alone and propositioned me about a sexual encounter. In this conversation, it was made known to Josh that I had to discuss this with my man, but I was curious.

Later that night, I spoke with my boyfriend, Eric, about the proposition from Josh. I felt that my man was the one that wanted the open relationship; I might as well test the waters. And when I say, "test the waters", I mean test out my man's response and see how this was going to play out with Josh, as I was curious about the white boy. With me being a black beauty, I didn't involve myself with the swirl… if you know what I mean. So I talked to my man and he asked me if I was sure. I said that I was, even though I was not truly sure if this was a door I wanted to open; but he is the one that wanted it, so I thought I would put that to the test.

Later that night, we took Josh back to our place and proceeded to get it on. It was me and two men. This was not my first encounter in a threesome. We will go more into detail about my first encounter a little later. While the three of us were getting down and dirty, it became obvious that Josh was like a third wheel. Yes, it began with me kissing and doing other sexual things to both of them, but it soon became clear that I didn't really want Josh. I was so much more interested in my own man that poor Josh was kind of left in the cold. I did not mean to make Josh feel like that; but with the way I was feeling, I just wanted my man to make me feel even better. Needless to say, the night ended quickly with us taking Josh back home, so that my man and I could go back home and finish what we started.

CHAPTER TWO

Let *me give a little more history about my man and me.* I met him in college and shortly after graduating, I found myself with no place to really go. I had moved back home with my mother for a very short time after graduation and that did not work out. For one, I had already been living on my own for four years. I was living by my own rules and now I found myself back in the home that I desperately tried to get as far away from as possible when I was a teenager. Secondly, my younger sister was murdered the same year that I graduated from college and my sister was obviously my mother's favorite; so when I went back home there was tension because we were both still grieving my sister's death and that led to unwarranted tension and disagreements. My mother and I almost got into a fist fight and I was so taken aback that I packed my few belongings and got in my car and left south Florida.

I went back to my college town where I knew someone would let me sleep on their couch or something. After staying with a girlfriend for about a month, I knew I could not live in that house anymore either. My girlfriend was pregnant, and she had a roommate that was pregnant, and the other roommate was a drug dealer and all of that. Plus, the house was the neighborhood party house so there was way too much going on in that house and I knew I had to go. I called my now boyfriend, Eric. He lived with another guy named Shawn, who I used to have sex with while we were in school.. Eric and Shawn were also in a fraternity that was the brothers to the sorority that I became a member of two years prior. I smoked marijuana with them regularly, back when we were in college. I asked Eric if I could come live with him and Shawn temporarily, until I found a job and was able to move out into my own place. Eric said that it was fine and that he just needed to run it by his roommate, Shawn.

The next day I moved to Eric and Shawn's place. It was cool because I had a friendship with both of them as individuals and together because we all used to hang out. Whenever I was able, I would get some ecstasy for myself and just chill at their house smoking and drinking. Eric and Shawn used to ask me about this ecstasy and how it made me feel. They wanted to know this because back in those days one ecstasy pill could cost $25 unless you knew the right people and could get it for much less. They wanted to know why I would spend so much on one pill when I could get a quarter of marijuana for the same price and it would last longer. I explained that the feeling that I got from rolling was so much more intense than if I smoked a blunt.

So, one day, I told them I was leaving to go get some "beans" which was a nickname people had for ecstasy. Eric gave me some money and asked me to get one for each of them (Eric and Shawn). I said of course and came back with beans and weed and a bottle of vodka. By the time I got back, Shawn was sleeping. I did not want to wake him, so I gave Eric his bean and we rolled up a blunt and smoked and drank while listening to music, and while Eric played video games. Now the bean was starting to kick in. When that happens, I want to take a hot bath because the hot water feels so good. While in the tub, I would put my vagina directly under the warm water while it was running because my clitoris was so sensitive and that made me almost climax just from the warm water. I felt so good and I would play with myself while this was going on also. I would be so ready for sex after this.

Anyway, I went and started a bath for myself; and Eric later asked if he could join me in the tub. I had no problem with that. I did not have a boyfriend and hell; they were letting me live rent free at their place. While we were in the tub together for the first time, Eric was obviously starting to feel good as well and he became touchy feely with me. I did not mind because it felt good.

While we were in the tub, we had a blunt that we were smoking and just relaxed while the music played. Shortly after we stopped smoking, Shawn walked in the bathroom looking confused. Both our naked bodies lay in the tub and we looked very happy. Shawn asked Eric "Is it worth the $25?" Eric replied, "It is worth it and better than any type of marijuana that you can buy." We all laughed and rolled another blunt.

The next time that I went and got some beans for all three of us the night played a little differently. As I earlier mentioned, I had a sexual relationship with Shawn when I was in school. We were never girlfriend and boyfriend. We had a casual sex relationship. We were like friends with benefits, in the past. This night, Eric, Shawn and I began to get very friendly with each other. I did as I always did; I went straight for the tub. Now the three of us were in the tub with our legs hanging over the edge because this was not a big Jacuzzi tub. It was a regular old tub with very little room. While in the tub, I had Eric on one side of me and Shawn on the other side. We were feeling our beans and our hands began to roam. I was feeling on both of them and they were feeling on me and I liked it. Shawn went in first and started kissing me. As we kissed, I felt Eric going for my lady hole. He was massaging me while Shawn kissed me. After I kissed Shawn, I turned and looked at Eric while he continued to massage me, and Eric began to kiss me while he massaged me. In my head, I kept thinking, *damn I really like this. It feels so good and I am definitely entering unchartered territory for myself. But I like it and I want it to continue.* Shortly after that, we got out of the tub and went into the living room. It was on and popping after that. I had one man in front of me and one man behind me and I was excited. We were standing in the middle of the floor kissing and touching and being sensual and to make it even better we played some Prince to keep the mood going.

This was the kind of scene that one would fantasize about, but I was living it. Shawn laid me on the couch and began to lick on my clitoris and suck on my vagina, my body moaned, and I looked over at Eric and fingered him over to me. I turned over so that Shawn could continue taking care of me and I could pull Eric to me and play with his manhood. Shawn was giving me great head from behind. I began to put my mouth on Eric's penis, and I went down as far as I could so that his penis was at the very back of my throat. I then came up very slowly because this guy I used to work with told me that men love when a girl gives them slow head.

The night went on with me in the middle of everything. Just call me Monie!!!! For me it was work because I had two men to please and make sure they were content while they sexed me up.

My hands and mouth were busy. It was a great experience and I don't regret a thing. This little experience happened some more while we all lived together which was not for long. We all lived together for about six months. After that, I moved to another city in Florida and Eric moved to the same city as I did shortly after. Shawn went somewhere in the mid-west.

CHAPTER THREE

Back to my man... Eric and I starting our own official relationship. We are now living in central Florida and living our lives. Our routine was simple. We would work during the week and when Friday came, the party was getting started. It got to the point that I grew a closer friendship with the person that I was getting the ecstasy from and the prices became really good. We would get all our "party favors" before Friday so when the weekend came, we could turn up, have fun and not have to make runs to the store or meet up with people to get our necessary drugs.

After that night with Josh, Eric and I were fine in our relationship. We enjoyed the evening and then went back to our regular lives. One day, it came to me. I said to myself that I would try to have threesomes with women who were bisexual so they could be interested in both Eric and me. I also thought that was a great idea because he would not feel any kind of insecurities in that type of setting. He would be pleased. I would be pleased. She would be pleased. Everybody would be happy. That is what I call a win, win, win situation. During our partying we would either go out to a club or just make the party at our house. Or go to someone else's house if they were having a shindig.

During these party weekends, we would encounter different people and different situations. During one of these weekends, we were at our apartment and I was downstairs at my car when I met a young lady and her little sister in the apartment complex. I said hello as they were walking by and we just instantly hit it off. We stood down there talking for a few minutes and then I went back upstairs to my apartment. When I got upstairs I told Eric about the young lady that I met while she was on her way to the store.

Eric said, "Why didn't you offer her a ride?" I said, "I didn't even think about that." I went downstairs and got in my car and drove through the parking lot to find this young lady. I found them walking and offered them a ride to the store. We talked in the car and I took them home after we left the store. As the young lady was getting out of the car, she asked me what I was doing tonight. I told her that some friends and I were hanging out at my house and she was more than welcome to join us. She said that she would like to join us, and she just had to get her sister back in the house with her mother.

The young lady came back to the car and I asked her, "What is your name?" as I laughed. She laughed as well and said, "My name is Tracy." I said, "Hello Tracy, my name is Stephanie. How are you doing?" I put my hand out to shake her hand and we both laughed all the way back to my apartment. We walked in and I introduced her to everyone and when I introduced her to Eric, he said, oh you found her, huh? We all cracked up laughing.

The party was on and we were all drinking and smoking. I told Tracy what we were on and she asked if we had any more. Of course I did, because I always bought in bulk. I usually got 20 - 30 pills a weekend because they went fast. Between me and Eric taking them and giving some to our friends that would come by, we could never have enough. The nights lasted for days. We would start on a Friday and not turn down until Sunday evening. This was the meaning of sex, parties and drugs all the time (really just on the weekends).

We were living like rock stars lived. Except one thing and that was that we didn't have the money or fame of a rock star. First, I asked Tracy if she had ever done ecstasy before and she said no. I asked if she was sure that she wanted to partake because I did not want any problems. She laughed and said that she was sure, so I gave it to her. It was obvious when she started to feel it, which was about 35 to 45 minutes later. Her body language changed, and she became very free from her facial expressions.

Eric began to also notice her change in demeanor. He pulled me to the side and asked me to see if she wanted to take a bath with us. I got her alone in the kitchen and mentioned that a warm bath would make her feel even better. I then offered her the opportunity to take a bath, but that I would be in it. She smiled really big when I said that I would be joining her in the tub. She seemed liked she was absolutely fine with that and so we got a nice warm steamy bubble bath going and we got in together. While she and I were in the tub, Eric shortly came in the bathroom and asked if he could join us.

I looked at her to make sure that she was ok with that. She looked at me with the same expression. It's like we both wanted to make sure that the other was fine with the question. We both nodded our heads in agreement. Eric then joined us in the tub. Eric was in the very back, Tracy was in front of Eric and he fondled her breasts and other body parts. I was in front of Tracy, but I was facing her and Eric. I began to lick Tracy's nipples very slowly.

She smiled. That was my cue that I could continue. With my hand palming her other breast, I slowly licked around her nipple and then placed the tip of my tongue gently over the nipple itself and moved my tongue up and down so that she could feel the roughness of the top of my tongue on it. She let out a soft moan and said, "Do that again." I followed her request. While palming her other breast and sucking on the breast in question, I moved my other hand down to her love hole. I placed my thumb directly on her clitoris and my finger inside of her. Her body motioned as if she were ready for what was about to happen. Still paying close attention to her breast, I began to rub my thumb around on her clitoris and massaged it gently.

What's funny is that I have never been here before with a woman. I was a little tickled at myself. I imagined how I would want my vagina to be touched and massaged and I did that to her. Tracy was obviously enjoying what was going on. Eric was behind her in the tub rubbing his hands all over the other parts of her body that I was not occupying. We continued this for a while. Switching from licking on her breasts to licking on her lips back and forth we went. We all felt good, we were all rolling on ecstasy. As I sucked on her breast and kissed her, I switched to the other breast and continued to massage her clitoris, moving my finger around inside her so that I could feel up inside of her g-spot. With my finger moving around at her g-spot and my thumb massaging her clitoris, she let out a cry of yes, yes, yes and she made somewhat of a squeal while this was going on.

Then she started to grab my breasts which were very large, and she put both of my nipples in her mouth at the same time and began to suck as if her life depended on it. I kept massaging her vagina but gave room for her to work on my breasts. While she worked on me, Eric took up the slack by going for her breasts and we all 3 were in the tub having a free for all and we loved every little bit of it. By now, all the guests that we had in our apartment had left and it was just the 3 of us. We moved from the tub to the bed. Drying each other off first, we each helped the other out until we were all dry. We got in the bed together.

Tracy went straight for me. She began sucking my breasts and placed her finger in my vagina. She rubbed my vagina for a while and then she threw my legs back behind my head and proceeded to lick and suck on my clit and sticking her tongue all the way inside of my vagina and began to penetrate it like it was a penis. I had adult toys and a couple of dildos that I would use sometimes. They were already out in the room, so she grabbed a dildo and inspected it. Then she put her mouth all over the dildo to get it wet. She then inserted the dildo into my womb. While she is fucking me with the dildo, she is also sucking in my clit. She spit in my clit and then sucked the spit off of it.

By now, Eric is playing with my breasts and touching Tracy. He is basically trying to get in where he can fit in. Tracy was fucking me so that I climaxed. While I climaxed I let out a squeal and that made her suck on me even harder which intensified the climaxing. I never came so hard in my life. I definitely wasn't expecting this outcome when we first met hours prior to this moment. I was so overwhelmed at having my own feeling of ecstasy.

When she was done, Eric laid her down on the bed and began to suck on her clitoris. While he was paying her back for the great head that she had just blessed me with, I laid underneath him so his penis could fit directly into my mouth. He fucked my mouth while he sucked on her and this was so sexy. I was so horny, and this position turned me on. I had dick in my mouth and pussy above my head. I felt like we were in a porno movie. This was one of the perks of being a grown up and be able to do whatever you want.

Eric was doing her real good because she came all in his mouth and he almost choked me because his penis was still in my mouth when he became stiff as a board and let out this loud moan. He grabbed me from underneath him after he was done pleasing Tracy and plowed his penis into my pussy. My pussy was dripping wet from being so hot and bothered. While Eric was sexing me down, my head was hanging over the bed slightly.

Tracy came over and put her pussy directly over my mouth while Eric fucked my brains out. I grabbed her ass and squeezed to hold on and have a grip to pull her pussy in as far into my mouth as it could get. She and Eric were kissing and fondling each other while I sucked her pussy and he fucked me. I mean to tell you that we all made sure to stay busy during all of this and it was great. I shifted my hips up because I felt myself about to climax. This made me squeeze Tracy's ass really tight and grab hold of her clit with my tongue.

All moaned and squealed at the same time and it seemed like we were all climaxing at the same time. We all made loud sex noises and then stopped to catch our breath. The three of us lay in the bed. Eric was in the middle of Tracy and me. we all laid there, breathing heavily, trying to catch our composure. Eric worked part-time at a restaurant on the weekends. The three of us had been going at it since late Friday night.

It was now early Saturday at about 7 am. Eric had to arrive at work at 8 am. Eric called his job and the cook of the restaurant happened to answer. The cook was one of the people whose house we would go hang out at sometimes and he indulged in some of the same party favors that we did. Eric proceeded to tell the cook exactly what his current situation was. Eric said, "Man I am laying in my bed between Stephanie and another female."

One could hear the big smile that Eric had on his face in his voice. He was in a place where most men wished they could be. I could hear the cook laughing through the phone as I lay next to Eric. The cook then stated, "So that means that you are not coming in today… right?" as he giggled. All that Eric could say was, "Man…. I don't know if I have the energy after what we all just did." The cook said, "You enjoy yourself dawg and I will let them know that something came up and you are not able to make it in today." Eric replied, "Thanks man I owe you, BIG!!!!!" We all indulged in each other some more that day, until Tracy parted ways with us later on Saturday night.

Now the weekend had past and it was back to work on Monday. We both went to work, as usual. The funny thing about me is that I am very professional when it comes to my job. No one that works with me could ever imagine the lifestyle that I have outside of work. I sometimes felt as if I were living a double life.

On one end I am high heels, business suits and delegation. I was a senior worker at a government office, so I had to keep a certain persona to make sure that the Caucasians that I worked for felt comfortable with promoting me in the future. I was good at my job. I did not plan on being there forever, but I wanted to make sure that I did the very best job that I could do while I was there.

My job was stressful at times because we had to deal with clients in person and that could get hectic when clients want things to go their way, as that is not always the outcome. Someone is not going to be happy. When our clients were unhappy with something, they showed it. I remember one particular day; I had a client that would not calm down, no matter how much I tried. The issue was so bad, that we ended having to call the police on this person because we felt like she would cause some danger to workers and other clients that were there.

When I got home that day, I told Eric all about my stressful day. While I talked, he rolled up a blunt. We had both had a hard day at work and just needed to unwind. We smoked and had some wine and just lay on the couch holding each other until we fell asleep. See we did not always have nights as fun filled as other nights. The thing I liked about Eric was that we partied when we partied and when it was time for business he understood for the most part. Sometimes I had to be the grownup of the relationship and remind him of what's important.

CHAPTER FOUR

Since that time period we have moved into another apartment with our now roommate, Alexander. We called him Alex for short. Alex was gay and he definitely lived the gay lifestyle. Alex's friends would come over to the house and chill with us on Friday nights when we were rolling on ecstasy or just hanging out. Being around the "queens" as we called them made me feel so free. It was usually gay men and I knew they didn't want me at all, so that made me act even more free.

When I would start feeling my bean, I would slowly come out of my clothes. Sometimes I was in the house butt-naked, or perhaps with just a thong on. The bean made things feel sensitive and also would warm me up. So when I got hot, I would just come out of what made me hot. One night, a couple of our friends came by the house. It was a male and female couple. They got really comfortable with us as well. We ended up having a little rendezvous after we all knew each other for some time.

Since we were both couples, I came up with rules. I didn't want there to be any funny feeling or animosity after the evening had passed. The rule was that either man could not penetrate the other guys female with their penis. Everyone could lick, suck, finger, touch, etc.; but when it was time for down and dirty sex-play both men had to penetrate their own woman. I felt that was enough for us to have fun but not take it too far. By this time in our lives; I had stopped working for the government and was working in the private sector. The job that I had in the private sector actually offered the opportunity for Eric and me to travel. One day, when I went into the office to turn in paperwork, the boss asked me if there was anything holding me in the city that I was in. I said no. I did not have any children; we were renting our apartment, so I was flexible. I could move about the country in any manner that I wanted.

The boss asked me if I would be willing to go to Rochester to work for six weeks. Before I could ask any questions about the logistics, my boss said, "We will pay for everything. You will be paid hourly and your room and board is covered. Plus, you will receive daily per diem and an additional check weekly for food and miscellaneous. We will fly you up there and everything is taken care of." I said well, I don't want to leave my car. I would rather drive it up. I wanted to drive my car because if I left it with our roommate, I might have come back to NO car!

Alex was a cool dude and he had a great sense of humor, but he was very clumsy. And he was a bit rough on vehicles. I told my boss that I would go home and discuss this with Eric. Even though Eric was not my husband, he was very important to me and I didn't want to just leave him hanging. I did make up my mind about going before getting home so I needed Eric to say yes because I wanted to go. I wanted to travel, and this was a great way to go somewhere for free. When I got home, I said to Eric, "Guess what?" Eric asked what I was talking about. I said, "Well, I was asked if I could travel with the company." Eric said, "What are you talking about?" I told Eric about the conversation with my boss and that I want to go to Rochester. I told Eric that I was really excited, and I needed him to be on board with it.

Eric had previously quit his job a month prior because he was sick of the people there and started doing what I was doing, so he knew exactly who I was talking about when I said my boss. I asked Eric "Is there anything keeping you here? We don't have any children and we are renting; we can just send money to Alex to pay our portion of the rent while we are gone. I mean it makes perfect sense for us to take advantage of this opportunity. We have nothing to lose, baby, come on. I really want to do this."

Eric was in careful thought for a moment and then he said, "You know what, F it, let's do it." Eric then asked, "Wait, what about your car?" I said, "I am driving, you know I can't afford to leave my car here with Alex. Isn't no telling what condition it will be in when I get back if it's running at all." We both laughed and were in agreement.

I called my boss and said we are in and requested the details. My boss told me to keep my gas receipts and they will reimburse me for gas and hotel on the way up. I told him that it was perfecta and we would prepare for our trip. We were to leave in a few days.

It's days later and we are on the road. We drove up to New Orleans and spent the night because Eric had family there. We went from New Orleans to somewhere in Ohio. It was a little rink dink hotel in Ohio, but we were trying to keep it inexpensive because we were balling on a budget. After two days of driving, we had finally made it to Rochester, NY.

I had never been to New York before. Even though it wasn't the city of New York, it was nice to be there. We were in upstate New York, which had some pretty scenery during the summer. We were there in July of that year. I could not have gone if it had been for the winter. I am a Florida girl and I don't really do well in the cold. I'm from where we wear tank tops and booty shorts because it's hot! Anyway, upon our arrival, we realized we ran out of marijuana, so we had to figure out a way to get some more. We figured it couldn't be that hard. We were in a major city where there were a lot of diverse people. We were at a hotel that we were put up in until the next day when our apartment would be ready. The hotel was part of a major chain and it was pretty busy with people in and out.

There was a restaurant and couple of stores and boutiques on the first floor. Eric and I were walking out of the hotel to go and smoke a cigarette and the last little roach that we had left with a very small amount of weed. While we were by the car, Eric hisses at me. He looked toward the hotel and said, "Her." He also spoke to me with his eyes, while he was hissing. I looked at him like what!!! What are you talking about? He said, "She looks like she may know where to find some weed." I just rolled my eyes. *Here we go,* I thought. "Ok and what do you want me to do about that?" He said, "go and inquire if she may know where we can get some." I said, "I don't want to go, you go!" He said, "You are a girl, it would look less incriminating if you approached her." Damnitt! He was right. No one would suspect a thing if I asked and she certainly looked as if she knew where to find it, even if she did not use it herself. Now all of this happened within seconds, so I had to move quickly.

She was a young lady, maybe about 25 to 27 years old. She was really jazzy. She had a short blonde haircut with a denim dress that was short, but not hoochie mama short, with some brown sandals to accent the denim. She was walking towards the door of the hotel from her car in the parking lot, not far from us. I caught her as she was about to walk in the door. "Excuse me, miss, excuse me! Hi, how are you? I am visiting in town from down south and I have a question, if you don't mind." She said, "No I don't mind, how I can help you?" I got closer to her and asked to move a little away from the door in a whispering type of voice. She moved over and asked, "What is it that you have a question about?" I leaned in close to her so that I could speak where only she and I could hear. I said, "Do you happen to know where I could get some trees from?" She looked at me weird. I said, "I promise I am not the police, but I don't know where to go around here." She said, "Girl, you can get arrested for this, you better be careful." I said, "I know, as you can see we are desperate." She said, "We!" I said, "Yes, my boyfriend and I drove up from Orlando and we are just trying to find out where to go because we will be here for a few weeks."

I waved to Eric to come over. The jazzy blonde-haired female just burst out in laughter while looking at our pitiful faces. She said, "I know this one place that my cousin goes to. I don't smoke like that, but my peoples do. Let me run in here for a moment and I will show you where it is." I replied, "Thank you so much. We are going to wait out here in the car until you are ready." She said "ok." When she returned, she waved for us to follow her after she got into her truck. We followed her to this neighborhood that looked like a typical up north neighborhood with the townhouses looking exactly the same and there were rows of them up and down the streets. Some of them were abandoned and some had lights on in them. We pulled up to one that was pretty dark, but it had a small amount of light in one room. We went to the back of the house to a window. She said her name as if to let them know who she was for familiarity. She then asked for two dimes. A young man maybe about 20 years old, opened the window and held out his hands with 2 dime sacks of weed. I gave her the money and she gave me the product. I said, "Thank you and have a nice night" to her and the young man at the window; and I went on about my merry little way. I got back into the car with Eric and off we went.

We spent more than six weeks in Rochester, doing work seeing the sites and taking advantage of being in a strange land. We went to Niagara Falls and we even went to the Canadian side and had dinner at a restaurant there, which was really nice. Niagara Falls was absolutely gorgeous. Especially considering the fact that I love waterfalls, big and small. I was happy to be there. During the time that we were working in Rochester, we ran into an issue. We were working for this billionaire that wanted to run for governor and he hired us to help him do that. Well, since that ruffled the feathers of the then governor at the time, that governor decided to sue each of us that came up to Rochester to work. That situation caused us to have to stay in Rochester for longer than expected, but that was fine because we were getting paid extra for our time and bonuses when it was all over.

One day, we all had to go to Albany to meet with attorneys and take depositions, so our boss decided to charter a bus for us to go to Albany and when we were finished with the depositions we could ride back to Rochester with liquor and food. It was like a party bus. We had a great time and the best thing about it was that we were being paid for all of it. We were even being paid to party. That was a great experience and when it was over, Eric and I took our money and our new car that we purchased with our earnings and we left New York State. That was one of the best times that I had in my life. We met a lot of different people from different races and cultures. It was great. Now Eric and I were back in Orlando and we had a whole bunch of cash. Of course we partied a little bit, but we were also waiting for another possible job with this company.

Open Marriage

Later that week we got the call for a job out west in Nevada. We were warned that this job would not be as glamorous and lavish as the other job. The person paying the company for this job was different, so they were not as forthcoming with taking care of our expenses. We had to pay for everything, but it was all good because we were going to make money and between the two of us, we would be fine. So that next week we were on the road, in our new car this time. We spent the night in Texas, and we spent the night in Las Vegas. We were headed up to Reno to work. Now by this time, Eric and I had been dating each other and living together for three years. While in Las Vegas, we spent the night at Eric's aunt's house.

We sat up talking with his aunt and uncle, and she mentioned that we were going to Reno and there was a wedding chapel on every corner. We both laughed and kept the conversation going. The next morning we were on the road. Finally hours later, over the mountains and through the hills, we made it to Reno, Nevada. The biggest little city in the US. We were assigned to work the outskirts of Reno which were mountain towns. Living in these little towns was very different. We even stayed in Carson City, where they filmed Bonanza back in the day. It was quite an experience.

Eric and I stayed out there for about eight weeks. When we were about three weeks in, I asked Eric, "Have you ever thought about us getting married?" He kind of froze in what he was doing. Keep in mind; he was driving at the time. He said, "It crossed my mind." I said, "What do you think about it?" he said, "Well, I don't know, it's not like our families are here." I said, we could elope and go home already married. He hesitated and then said, "Are you sure?" I said, we have been together for three years and I don't really see myself with anyone else except you, especially after all that we have been through."

It was quiet in the car and I was starting to feel a little irritated. I am feeling that if our ultimate goal isn't marriage, then what we are together for. After that conversation it was a cold and silent car ride back to the hotel. We walked into the hotel room and I went straight to the bathroom and took a shower and put on my pajamas and got in the bed. Obviously, I had an attitude. *I mean... really, am I not worth being married to? What the hell does he take me for? Am I supposed to just shack up with him until he feels like marrying me or leaving me to marry someone else? I don't know what the hell he takes this for.* All of these were the thoughts in my head. Eric said something to me, and I totally ignored him.

By this point, he could kick fucking rocks. I was pissed. Not even has he not thought to propose to me, but when I bring it up, he comes back with all the reasons why he feels we shouldn't get married. Fuck him, when we get back to the east coast it's over, he can kiss my ass. I am not going to be bothered with someone who doesn't even think highly enough of me to want to make me their wife. Fuck him fuck him fuck him!!!!! After he got out of the shower, he got into the bed and asked me if I really wanted to get married. I just ignored him. Obviously not, if you don't want to. We are certainly not on the same page and we don't need to be together if we don't have the same goals and similar aspirations for where this relationship is going. I went to bed pissed. I fell asleep mad and wanted nothing else to do with him.

The next morning, I woke up thinking about exactly what it was that was on my mind the night before and that was this bullshit about us getting married. At first, I was a little excited that we could possibly be getting married, but now it has just pissed me off more and more. I am so upset that I don't know what to do with these feelings. I laid there in the bed with my eyes open, but I didn't move my body because I didn't want him to know that I was awake. He might want to try and have a conversation and I was not ready to talk to him. As I lay there, he rolled over and held me and began to talk. I'm saying to myself that he must have some type of Spidey sense to know that I was awake because I had not moved an inch. He must be able to hear my thoughts. He said, "Baby let's get married."

I was still salty and didn't say anything. On the inside I was happy, but I knew that he was only saying this because I got so upset with him the night before about this topic. So now this leaves me with the question of, is he just saying this so that I won't be mad at him anymore or does he really find me worthy enough to marry? I was so confused at this point because I did not know how to react. I laid there trying to get my thoughts together.

At this point I was in my mid-twenties. Knowing that I wasn't getting any younger, I did think about it. The expectation was instilled in me that I was supposed to go to college and meet my husband while in college; so in my mind, we were supposed to be together because the situation fell into the expectation that I had on marriage, and how and where I was to meet my husband. With a stankin attitude, I rolled over and said, "Why would you want to marry me?" I was waiting for his answer so I could dissect it and curse him out for whatever the response would be, just because he hurt my feelings and really made me upset.

His response was not what I was expecting at all. "He said I want to marry you because you are a beautiful person. You are my ride or die chick and I don't know where I would be if I did not have you in my life. Even at this point, we don't know what the future holds, but I know that my future is bright as long as I have you by my side. I didn't ask you those questions last night to make you upset. I just want to make sure that you really want to do this, and you are not just falling into the excitement of there being a wedding chapel on every corner. I also wanted our families to be present when we say I do, especially because my mom was not able to make it to my sister's wedding and if we elope she will miss out on my wedding also. However, I do love you and I don't see myself with anyone but you, so will you give me the honor of being my wife?"

I was so stubborn, I was sitting up in the bed looking at him with my eyes rolling and trying to look as nonchalant as possible, even though I was very excited on the inside, I could not show him my true reaction. Not just yet. He had to suffer. My response was simply, "I will think about it!" He said, "Oh Really!" I said, "yes really," he began to tickle and kiss me to break down some of the tension that I had built up. It worked. He knows me well enough to know how to get me to let my guard down when I am being stubborn because I sometimes ride that wave of stubbornness until there is nothing left. We both laughed and kissed very passionately. He asked me the question again and this time when he asked, I hugged him and said yes very softly while

I stopped kissing him for a moment to utter those words and continued kissing him.

I was happy, but there was still some uncertainty in the back of my mind. I was not uncertain that I wanted to be married to him. I was somewhat uncertain about him wanting to be married to me because of this entire ordeal that we had just encountered over the last 24 hours. We got up and got prepared for a day of work. After some time, we actually began to make preparations to be married. I was excited. Even though my family wasn't there, I felt like we were doing the right thing. We found a chapel to have the ceremony and there was a nice hotel directly across from the chapel. I was very big on hot tubs and Jacuzzis and their master suite had a hot tub in the room, so that was perfect for me. That would help the "Honeymoon" night to be very romantic.

We went to a florist and got my favorite flowers at the time, which was sunflowers. I felt somewhat like a young hippie. We had a chapel and the arrangements were made for after the ceremony. We were very tight on money, so we definitely had to be considerate of our budget. We went to get wedding rings and I purchased a cute little off-white dress that fit over my little petite frame perfectly. By now, we had everything in order and were just waiting for the actual day that this was going down.

Meanwhile back in the hotel room that we were staying in for the work that were out there doing, Eric came to me. He said, "Baby, I know we have a lot going on right now and soon things will be changing for us. I want to make sure that I do this correctly." I was sitting on the side of the bed looking at him while he was talking.

Eric was not facing me when he was talking at first. He then turned around and said, "I want to make sure that we do this right." Eric got down on one knee and said, "It will make me the happiest man on this Earth if you would be my… Stephanie, will you marry me?" I sat there smiling. "Of course, baby, I will marry you." He smiled and I smiled, and we hugged and kissed each other as if we knew that this was going to be a journey. What we did not know was how much of a roller coaster that our lives together would be.

The day had arrived, and it went off without a hitch. We were in front of the minister with our boss, one of our coworkers and one of our boss's daughters as witnesses to our special day. We were so young. Looking into each other's eyes, wondering what the other was thinking. I know that I was thinking, *Are we really doing this, am I really ready to be with the same person for the rest of my life, my goodness what am I doing?* Ok Stephanie, calm down, you got this, everything will be fine, and you guys will be happy, you will see.

After going through all of the thoughts in my mind, I really started to wonder what type of thoughts that he was having. Was he having doubts, was he happy about this decision, was he really content to being with me for the rest of his life????? I had so many questions and this was not the time to bring them all up. The arrangements had been made, people were in place and somebody was getting married today. So, the minister is at the part where they ask the question. Stephanie, do you take Eric as you lawfully wedded husband, to have and to hold through sickness and in health, yada, yada….. And it was now or never. "I Do!"

"Eric, do you take Stephanie to be your lawfully wedded wife to have and to hold …...? Eric let out a silent pause. We all stared at him, like will you answer the question. Eric choked for a moment then said, "I do" and that was it, ladies and gentlemen. We had officially moved from boyfriend and girlfriend to husband and wife. Wow, this was going to great. Our lives were going to be wonderful. This was a good thing. And now with God tying us together, along with the state of Nevada, we were officially Mr. and Mrs. Eric Johnson.

Open Marriage

We all went to dinner afterwards at my favorite Italian restaurant at the time and we drank wine and had tiramisu as our dessert / wedding cake. The night was beautiful and when dinner was over with, it was time for the honeymoon. We said goodnight to our friends, bid them adieu and went back to our suite.

Now if you have learned anything about me, so far one thing that you will notice is that I love warm baths with bubbles, candles and wine, especially when it is in a Jacuzzi. So we had the entire fixings, wine, weed, bubbles and us. We did not have ecstasy this time because we were so far away from home. It was one thing finding weed when you are in a strange land, but ecstasy is on a totally different level and people look at you funny. They look at you like you are a drug addict or something when all we want to do is enjoy each other to the tenth power. Anyway, it was another ordeal finding marijuana while we were out in Nevada.

Once again, I was the pawn. Eric and I were trying to figure out where we were going to get more trees from because we had run out of what we traveled with. Eric says, "Let's go to a smoke shop. As soon as we see someone buying the little jewelry bags, we will approach them." That was a great idea that Eric proposed. So we go to our nearest smoke shop, thanks to the yellow pages, which is unheard of nowadays, but that is how we found information before Google. Anyway, we go into the smoke shop and we are looking around at the different pipes and all the types of smoking paraphernalia, which was really cool to tell you the truth.

While browsing, Eric noticed a young black male, maybe in his mid-twenties, going directly to the person behind the counter and asking for a certain size of the jewelry bags. The young man requested a large amount of these bags. Immediately, Eric nudges me. He says, "Go holler at him when he leaves the store." I looked at him and said, "Why can't you go talk to him? I did it last time." Eric said, "Because you are a fine-ass pretty girl approaching him. He is not going to have a problem stopping and talking to you because he is going to think that you are trying to holler at him. Plus you have big boobs and you will definitely have his attention." I rolled my eyes at Eric and said, "This is some bullshit." Then I whispered, "Fine" to Eric as I walked away heading towards the door to talk to the young man as he was leaving the smoke shop.

Once we both were outside more into the parking lot, I yelled out "Excuse me sir!" The young man turned around and looked in my direction. He said, "Are you talking to me?" I said, "as a matter of fact, I am," with a huge smile on my face. The young man was actually a nice-looking handsome dude so that made it a lot easier for me to flirt a little while I made the inquiry that I needed. I walked up to him to get closer and use some body language to help him be a little more comfortable, which helped me to be more at ease. I said, "Excuse me sir, yes I am talking to you. How are you?" flashing my big beautiful winning smile at him. He said, "I am fine and how are you doing, sexy?" I blushed a little and said, "I am doing well, thanks for asking." He said, "is there something that I can help you with?" I said, "Well I am glad that you asked me that question because there is absolutely something that you can do to help me."

He looked a little confused, while still smiling. I said, "I noticed you were grabbing some jewelry bags from inside the store. Were you getting them to put jewelry inside of them?" He said, "Not really, what are you getting at?" I said, "Well I am new in town, visiting, and I was trying to find some trees because I have run out of my stash and you look like just the person that can help me out with my dilemma." He smiled and said, "yes it is possible that I may know how to help you out with your dilemma." I said, "Great, I don't have cash on me now but what is your number and I will call you a little later after I get back to my hotel?" We exchanged numbers and then I asked, " what do you have anyway, nicks, dimes?? So I know what to have prepared when you come by." He said, "I have dimes." I said, "Ok, I will call you later." He said, "Make sure you call Me," as he smiled. I said, "True dat!!! I got ya number!" We both laughed and parted ways.

Later that evening, I called him and told him where I was staying. Before he came to the room, we put all our stuff up and out of sight and Eric waited in the bathroom so the guy would not feel uncomfortable. When the guy got there and knocked on the door. I let him in, and he stood by the door. I was honest with him once he came in. I said, "I want to be honest with you. I am here with my boyfriend, just so you know. Can I see what you have?" The guy passed me a small bag that was the size of a nick. I said, "You said you had dimes, this looks like a nick." He said, "Smell it." I smelled it and it was the fresh smell of sweet cheebah. I smiled and said okay. "How much?" He said "$20". I said, "That's kind of steep, but that's cool." I passed him the money and the tension seemed to go down in the room. I said, "My boyfriend is waiting in the bathroom. I am going to have him come out now if that's cool." The guy said, "It's cool" and we all laughed after I told Eric to come out. The guy said, "That's why I am standing at the door because I am like… I don't know ya' ll, so I needed to make sure that everything was good." I laughed and said, "I feel ya because I put everything away, just in case, because I was like… I don't know this dude and I don't want any problems." He laughed, and Eric and I laughed and that was the beginning of a great relationship. That guy became our weed man while we were out west in Reno. He was cool too. He was fine with meeting us wherever we were. I guess he worked with us because he knew we were from out of town.

Back to our honeymoon night. Eric and I were in the bubble bath, smoking weed and drinking wine. We were getting comfortable so that we could relax and really enjoy each other on this night. The night that we got married. It was so surreal at the time because I was now a married woman. Eric complained that I liked the water too hot so every once in a while he would sit on the side of the tub to cool off from the hot water.

Tonight when he sat on the edge of the tub, I began to massage his thighs and legs while I slowly led up to his male part. I was very happy and in a very sexual mood. One thing about me is that it doesn't take much to get me into a sexual mood. I am a lover of love and feeling good sexually falls right into that. I grabbed his penis in both of my hands and began to go up and down his shaft with my hands. While moving up and down with my hands, I took one of my hands and went down to his balls and began to play with his balls while I had his penis in the other hand. I stared at his penis while I played with it and all of these sexual thoughts began to come into my mind. I was admiring his penis while I continued to move his balls around in my other hand.

The anticipation was killing me, but I never wanted to rush and shove his penis into my mouth. I wanted to be a tease because I feel that the tease was a part of the fun and the turn on when it came to giving oral sex to a penis. I licked my tongue along the vein that runs outside of the penis. The vein throbbed as I slowly licked it. I learned a few things about what guys like when receiving oral sex from Eric back when I first introduced him to ecstasy. Eric told me that the vein on the male gender is very sensitive and that the skin that is directly underneath the tip is super sensitive. Naturally, I make sure to pay extra special close attention to those parts while providing oral sex to him. I also like to put the entire penis in my mouth and push it in until it hits so far in the back of my throat that I may gag a little. It creates a lot of saliva and makes it feel really good to him when he is receiving great head, as I provide.

While in the tub I am licking the vein of his penis and still moving his balls around in my hand. Now I am ready to dive in or let him dive in if I want to put it correctly. I grabbed his thighs with both hands and put his entire penis in my mouth without using my hands so I could just use my tongue as leverage while I sucked on it. Plus it turns me on to grab him and pull him in closer when I am sucking on him because I want to taste every morsel of him while we are engaging in sexual activity. While we were having a good time, it made me very horny and then I let go of his thighs so I could use my hands to jack his penis while my saliva gave it a sloppy wet lubrication that was sexy and nasty at the same time. While I played with his manhood, he was playing with my tittles and pinching and lightly biting parts of my body where his mouth could reach. I was jacking him off so good that I forgot that I wanted the night to last, so I didn't want him to climax just yet. I needed that inside of me.

I slowly began to end this oral sex segment of the night and we moved over to the couch that wasn't far from the Jacuzzi tub. On the couch, he was sitting up and I sat on top of him facing him. I teased him while slowly coming down on his penis but stopping short of him getting inside of me before I finally sat all the way down on his penis. I held the back of the couch to have leverage while I rode his dick. I went up and down and made sure to roll my hips around while I went up and down. I wanted him to get the full feel of my pussy wrapped around his love. I also wanted to make sure that I could go up as far as I could without his penis coming out and force my way down hard and fast, so he certainly felt those pussy muscles working.

I wanted him to enjoy the ride as much as I was enjoying the ride. So up and down I went for a while. I then turned around and rode his dick from behind, holding onto the coffee table that was in front of me, I grinded and twerked on his dick while my titties were smacking against his knees because of the position. I wanted to work his ass. He was going to remember this night. While I was riding him, he had a hold of my hips and was helping me to throw my pussy at him until I heard him let out this strong moan. While he moaned, he grabbed my hips extra tight and then I felt warm creaminess inside of me. Now, for most, this would be the end of the session, the warm creaminess made my pussy get wetter and now I was riding his just ejaculated penis which is very sensitive and all I heard was wait, no, oh, hold on, oh shit, I can't, time out, pause, girl!!!" And he grabbed my hips to make me stop because if he hadn't I would have kept going. We went a couple more rounds that night and to bring in the first night of being husband and wife. Then the next day, it was back to business.

We stayed out west for a few more weeks. We actually took advantage of being on the other side of the country, since we were both from the east coast. One thing we realized being in the mountain towns working was that it gets very cold out there. We were so not prepared for the weather. We thought we were going to be in the desert and hot. No, no, no. we were out there until October, so the temperatures were very low at night and some of the days. One day while we were working, someone told us that it was snowing two towns over from where we were. This was different for this Floridian raised girl. We actually enjoyed seeing a different way of living and animals just roaming free. In Carson City, horses just walked around like everybody else.

When we finished our work in Reno we went to visit our boss and his family in Oregon. We left Reno and drove over to San Francisco to spend the night. The hotels were a little pricey so we drove to a town over and got a hotel, then drove back to San Francisco the next day so that we could go and see the Golden Gate Bridge. We parked and walked out to the bridge and looked at its beauty. It was gorgeous, looking at the bridge and the way that it draped over the bay. I was also in awe looking at the city from this side and really paying attention to the large mountain that this city was on and operated on.

This was so different. I am from a place where everything is flat. Another thing about San Francisco that was very different is the way that the streets were made. Whether going uphill or downhill, each street flattened out at each intersection. There was no way to go straight down really fast without crashing your car into the street. After we left San Francisco, we drove up the highway which went up the west coast along the water. As I was driving, I noticed the beautiful rock and water formations. Oh my goodness, they were so immaculate. Some of them looked like lagoons and places that you would see on islands in the Caribbean, but this beauty was right here in the United States. This moment made me feel proud to be a part of this country and all of its splendor.

As we drove north on this highway we also ran into the redwood forest. Initially, when we came up on these trees it was dark, and I did not notice how huge the trees were. Eric was in the passenger seat making these noises because I was cruising pretty fast in the dark. All of a sudden there was a fork in the road in front of me, but this was no ordinary fork in the road. There was a necessary fork because there was a tree in the middle of the highway that was so huge they had to build streets around it because they were not cutting that sucker down. As I drove up closer to it, I said, "What in the world is that!" Eric said, "Baby, I have been over here praying that you would slow down because you obviously do not know these humongous trees that we are driving by. So baby could you slow down a little so that we make it out of here alive?" I said no problem as I was a little terrified at what I had just seen myself.

Shortly after that, we stopped and got a hotel so we could get some rest. The next day, we drove back over to this forest so that we could see these trees in the daylight. Oh my goodness!!!!! These trees we HUGE!!!! We had to take three pictures of one tree to get the full tree on film. They even had one tree carved out in the bottom so that visitors could drive their cars through the tree and take pictures. These trees were immaculate. I had never seen anything like this before in my life. I overheard another visitor say that the trees looked like God's toothpicks. After we finished viewing the trees, we were headed north until we finally made it to Oregon.

It was very nice there and the people that we met were really cool. And the best part was that everyone we met smoked weed. That was perfect. We definitely took advantage of being on that end of the country. After a few days in Oregon, it was now time to head back to our side of the country. So we were off and on the road again. We put so many miles on that new car of ours, but it was all well worth it. We really experienced a lot and it was a perfect way to start our new life together. On our way back we stopped at the Grand Canyon and basked in the glow of its beauty, as well. Another one of God's creations that absolutely took my breath away. I thought that I was going to see this hole in the ground, but it was far from just some hole. You could feel the stillness and the peace of just standing out there basking in the glory of awesomeness.

I was so taken aback by what I was seeing because it was not at all what I was expecting. Absolutely gorgeous. Seeing all of these sights on the way back home, plus seeing the Hoover Dam and getting to see plateaus like I learned about in school when we drove through New Mexico was just a wonderful experience and I would not trade any of that for anything in the world. This Earth is beautiful and God new exactly what he was doing when he created each part of it. Now with all of this driving we had to make sure our car was in good condition. After we left the Grand Canyon, I went to sleep and let Eric drive. I had done most of the driving because Eric's driver's license was suspended at the time and we did not want any mishaps. So I went to sleep to get some rest while Eric drove.

The Grand Canyon was in Arizona. By the time I woke up, we were in Texas. Eric had driven all through the night and the car had been going for almost 24 hours straight. We stopped at a place so we could get an oil change on the car because we had definitely put several miles on this vehicle of ours. While we were in the waiting room waiting for the car to be serviced, we could hear the mechanic that was working on it to give it an oil change. All we heard was a loud "Ouch! This thing is hot. How long were you driving?" Eric and I said in unison, "We just came from the Grand Canyon," while we laughed. The mechanic said, "Man this is the hottest I have ever had to deal with" as he continued to work on the car. We left the car mechanic and were back on the road until we reached New Orleans. Remember, this is where Eric's mother lived so we stopped there for some time to figure out our next move.

By now, our old roommate Alex had moved someone into the room where we were to help him with the rent and take the burden off of us. We were pretty much homeless, but not really. We stayed in New Orleans for a while a decided we would go ahead and set up shop there. It should not take long for us to find jobs and we could just stay with Eric's mom and her husband until we found a place and moved on our own. Things are still looking good and we will soon figure this out.

CHAPTER FIVE

A month into living in New Orleans, Eric found work at a newly opening restaurant, which is where he had plenty of experience. I was a college graduate and for some reason it was harder for me to find work. I went to the stores and the mall and everyone told me that I was overqualified. I applied to state and government entities and I only heard from one agency. I had to take a test for them before I could make it to an interview. This was so discouraging. Plus now our parents were asking us what our plans were now that we are married. This was coming from his mother and my mother. We were both feeling the same. We didn't have a plan; we just wanted to be together. Why do we have to have a plan to be married?

We were stressed because there were now expectations of us that we did not know how to fulfill. And to top it off, the sex life between Eric and I had changed. I complained to Eric in the past about not wanting to have sex unless we were intoxicated. However, in the past, we could get something to get the party started and I was guaranteed to have some love before the night was over. Now that we were living in New Orleans, we didn't know anyone with the type of party favors that we were used to. Plus if we knew people, we could not really do much while living in his mother's home except for smoking weed. She understood that we smoked and was fine with that.

This took a toll on our sex life and I was not a happy camper. One day we got into a very heated argument. I mean, we had some fights prior to this, but this was a big one and when we were finished yelling and screaming at each other, I slammed the front door and stormed out of the house. I knew at that moment that I was not going to make it living in such close quarters to his mom. Especially with me not having my own. I was very independent and not having a job and having to depend on Eric for everything was not pleasing to me. I couldn't take this. I needed my own. I had visited my best friend in North Florida a few months prior and I knew that she needed a roommate.

This city was some hours away from New Orleans where we were living. I talked to Eric and told him that I was not happy. I did not like living with his mother. I wanted to go. I was not really prepared for all of this. I asked him how he would feel about me going to Florida. Hell it wasn't like we were having sex with each other. Here we are, two months into this marriage and now I am miserable. I would never have thought that this is where we would be this soon. As we discussed our relationship, Eric asked, "Do you think we jumped into the marriage too quickly? You know we could get it annulled." I was a little upset by his statement. I said, "You know what, Eric, I don't care what you do because you obviously don't want to be married, if you are already talking about an annulment. That's fine, do what you are going to do. I am leaving. Since you don't really want to be married to me anyway, there is no need for me to stay here. I'm going to Gainesville."

I threw my wedding ring at him as I left the area that we were talking in. I went into the room and started packing my stuff. He said, "Where are you going?" I said, "You don't want me, and you have shown me that, so there is really no reason for me to stay. I'm leaving." Eric said, "Baby wait, please just sleep on it and if you still feel the same way, then I won't stop you after today." I said, "Fine, I will wait until tomorrow." Eric's mother came and talked to me later that night. She was trying to calm me down and reassure me that Eric loves me and that we should work on our relationship because we are now married, so we cannot just give up on it that easily. I told her that I thought our relationship would get better once we got married because a lot of times the only sexual encounters we would have were when we were high, and I wanted to feel wanted and loved by him and not just when he was high. She told me that when she married her first husband, who was Eric's father, she married him for the same reason. She thought that marriage would fix their relationship. It made me feel better to know that I wasn't alone in my expectation of marriage; but I was still feeling emotional and uncertain about what to do because this was not going how I wanted it or expected it… and I didn't like this.

After some time and thought I decided to leave for Florida. I did not leave the next day. I waited for some of the jobs that I had applied for to respond to me, to see if maybe I could get a job. Maybe that could help me to not feel this way. After a couple of weeks, I heard nothing. I even applied at the place where Eric was now working, and I had not gotten any response back from them either. After the holidays came and went, I moved to Gainesville in January of the following year. I knew that if I went back there that I could find a job faster and get on my feet. Gainesville is what I called my original stomping ground. This is the place where I learned my true self and where I became a woman and had to make real woman grown- up decisions. Please understand, that I had some very important decisions to make prior to leaving my hometown as a child that would shape the life that I grew to call my own. However, in Gainesville, I was officially on my own as an adult. Of course, I had the support of my mother and relatives because I was there for college, but the everyday decisions on how to make it and how I carried myself was all left up to me. I would create my own destiny. This is the place where I learned more about the party life than any other era in my life. I started smoking marijuana, cigarettes, doing ecstasy and other drugs when I moved to the college town where I grew up and knew to be home for many years.

So, after discussing this with my husband, Eric, I decided that I was going to go back to Florida because this New Orleans bull just was not working for me. I needed to feel free and independent and I could not when I felt alone. Even with a husband, I felt alone. He didn't understand me, and it felt that he understood me less after we were married, which did not make any sense to me. I guess I should have really looked at the bigger picture then. I moved back to my old stomping ground. Back to where I could get any party favors that I wanted. I could be amongst friends and people that I knew. I wasn't cooped up in the house with my mother-in-law all day. It felt refreshing to be away from Eric and his mother for a while. I was starting to feel like the walls were closing in when I was in NO.

So now, I'm back in Florida and I want to relax. I immediately began to look for work, but while I was waiting for responses from applications, it wouldn't hurt to get some beans. As a matter of fact, since I had been gone, my friend had become very close with someone that had beans and my friend would provide them at times. That was all that I needed to put a smile on my face. I needed a little bit of my life back that I had prior to Eric and me beginning this journey together.. It took a couple of weeks, but I was able to start training with this company that sold products. There was a $100 sign on bonus to start working with them, so I was on board because I needed cash. I was broke and looking for money by any means necessary, short of doing illegal business. I worked with that company for 2 weeks and realized it wasn't going to work out. I did not want to sell products door to door for a living. I did door to door sales living in Orlando and I was not ready to go that route again. Although it was great exercise, I needed stable income.

Why was it so hard for me to find work with a college freaking degree? This made no sense. Growing up I was told to go to college and get a degree so that I could get a good job. Okay. I did that. I went to college. I completed college, which by the way was a major achievement because a lot of people that came to school with me or that I met in college did not graduate. As a matter of fact, Eric did not have a college degree. When I met him, he was the vice President of the Black Student Union and was very prim and proper. He dressed very well and was very articulate and all about black power. Somewhere between his junior and senior year he just lost his motivation. He got arrested for something very dumb and spent 15 days in jail. After that, it seemed that everything went downhill. He started hanging out with these guys that sold drugs and began making runs for them to make money. It's as if Eric lost any bit of ambition that he ever had when he went to jail. I even tried to encourage him to go back to school, but he was very disinterested.

Anyway, back to me, I was back to being moneyless after that $100 bonus was gone. I didn't have to pay any bills immediately when I moved in with my friend because she knew my situation. We had been friends for 5 years and when I say that we have been through a lot together, it would be an understatement. She and I have held each other down when everyone gave up on us, as individuals and as a team. She lived with me for some time when I was in college because of her own personal issues that she was having, so we definitely have a loyalty between us.

After my little hot $100 was gone, I was in a desperation mode. I began to drive some time for the person that had the beans. He needed someone to take him out of town to pick up his stash and bring them back. I started telling him that I was available to drive for him because I knew he would pay me for it. So my life consisted of driving for the dope boy and submitting applications daily via the internet and in person to find a job. I was so uncertain of what life had in store. I thought that this was so different than the feelings that I had when Eric and I were saying "I Do" to one another. This cannot be how my life is going to be. What was the point in going to college? I could have just stayed home and got a job.

Then it quickly hit me. I could have never stayed at home with my mother. We would have killed each other. I reminded myself that I am a strong woman and I will get through this once I figure out what my next move would be. A few days after, I had this build myself up conversation with myself. One of my other friends that also lived in the same house said that he had a surprise for me. I asked him what he was talking about. He said he would tell me later. A few more days after that, my guy friend that spoke of the surprise asked me to take him to the bus station because he was leaving for a few days and needed a ride to the bus station. I was fine with that because I did have the car that Eric and I purchased while we were in New York. I was fine with running errands for my friend and her roommate, who happened to be a guy friend of mine that I met while in college.

My guy friend and I pulled up to the bus station and he got out of the car. I thought I was just dropping him off, but when he got out of the car, he asked me to wait for him to make sure his ticket was straight. Just in case he wasn't able to leave at that time. I told him that it was fine and that I would wait for him. He knows I am not the type of person that would leave anyone stranded. While I am sitting in the car waiting for my guy friend to come and let me know that he is good and that I can leave him, I notice a familiar face walking out of the train station. It was Eric!!!

Eric had come to Gainesville. Why was Eric in Gainesville? We have been talking daily and he did not say anything about coming into town. What is going on? I was surprised and happy at the same time. Although I was ready to get away from Eric and his mama by the time I left him, I was very ecstatic to see my dear sweet darling husband. That just rolls off the tongue. My husband. He walked over to the car where I was already standing outside. Then I realized who it was. My baby. I was so happy to see him. Now all I wanted to do was tear his clothes off. *How bad is this? My mind is always in the gutter. I am like a man in that way. I always have to keep a lot of my thoughts to myself for fear that people will look at me strange. I am a lover of love, emotional, physical, spiritual, and everything in between.*

Open Marriage

As Eric walked up, we began kissing very passionately. It had better be passionate. We had not seen each other in about a month so my juices were flowing, and I am sure he was ready as well. The best thing about him being here with me is the freedom that we were able to regain with each other. It just felt like we were so restricted when we were living with his mom. After we stopped kissing for a couple of seconds my guy friend was standing on the other side of the car. He looked at me and said, "Do you like your surprise?" We all just laughed.

My guy friend was named Ken. Ken and I became friends when I was a sophomore in college. We would hang out and smoke with each other. I knew early in our friendship that we could never date each other intimately. I observed the way that Ken moved in his relationships and how badly he would piss off his girlfriends, so I always kept it platonic. Our friendship works because he is that male that I can talk to when I need a man's opinion about something. I also know that he will be honest and not spare my feelings. We were all in the car headed back to the house where I was staying with Ken and my female friend that I discussed earlier. Claudia, my female friend was really like my closest friend at the time. As we pulled up to the house Claudia was standing outside with a bottle to greet us. As I got out of the car I said to her, "What is that?" She said, "DO you like your surprise homey???" I said, "Oh, so you were in on this too huh?" She said, "Absolutely!" Laughing, I said, "Well, cool."

Hugs were being passed around because Eric was friends with them as well … he knew them through me. Because Ken and Claudia were my closest friends, it was natural that he would know them and have his own relationship with each of them. That night, we had a great time. We drank, smoked, rolled on ecstasy; it was like the old days. I was elated and so happy to be able to have a good time with my man again, the way that it used to be. Some other friends of all of ours came through and it was like a big party. There were a couple of female friends of Ken's that would frequent the house and they were there that night. One of the girls was very pretty. She was from the Philippines and she was beautiful. She definitely commanded the attention in the room when she came around. I won't say that I was jealous, but I was definitely used to being the female that gets all of the attention in the room, wherever I went. It was good meeting this young lady when I arrived, but now I am introducing her to my husband, and I made sure to pay attention to and observe the body language upon their meeting. Maria was her name and she was cool. We had no problems, but I knew I had to pay close attention to interactions. That night continued through until the next morning. One thing about rolling on ecstasy was that it will keep you up all night. Everyone was cozy with each other. Rolling does that. Eric and Maria got to know each other, but nothing inappropriate. They both shared the same birthday and had some things in common. I could tell that he was attracted to her, but as long as he didn't act on that feeling, we were good.

One thing about me is that sleeping is my pastime. I enjoyed sleep. I never had a problem with working and doing what is necessary to take care of house and home, but when it was time to sleep, that is exactly what I did. As the sun came up I went and lay down. I left everyone and went and lay down in the bed because I was worn out from all of the excitement and partying. It was perfect because this was the weekend and that allowed time before the job search started up again. We enjoyed the rest of the weekend relaxing and having lights drinks and maybe a blunt or two.

It was Monday and the party was over. Both Eric and I were on the hunt. I went and got us newspapers so that we could search in the classifieds and see what type of work was out there. Eric had restaurant experience, so it did not take him long to go to some of the restaurants in the neighborhood and eventually land a job in the first week of his arrival. This pissed me off so much. I am feeling like what in the world had I accumulated the loans for if no one was going to hire me with my college degree.

This sucks. I was happy that Eric found work, but this was eating away at my spirit. But hey, I had to keep pushing. I knew that if I kept trying, that something would eventually give way to a job. I had already applied to the government agency that I was working for before and waiting for them to respond. They had to hire me because I knew how to do the job. One day Eric comes to me and tells me about a job opening at a retail store that he used to work at when we were in school. He said that he went in to find out more about it and realized that the manager was the person that was his manager when he worked there. He talked to her and the next day I went in and filled out the application.

I was interviewed on the spot. In my mind, this was a good thing because I did really well at interviews. I just had to get to the interview. That is something that I was not able to do with any of the other hundreds of applications that I submitted all over. During the interview, I smiled, articulated my words, gave good eye contact and answered all of the questions that the person asked. The interviewer was another manager that worked during the day. He asked me about my work history and my goals and skills. When the interview was complete, I felt very good and knew that I was going to get this job. There was one little thing that took me by surprise. The manager said, "I think you are a good fit for this position. There is one more thing I need from you and then we can get you started." I said, "Okay, no problem. What else do you need from me?" He said, "I need you to go take a drug test. Once that test comes back we can get you hired." I smiled and said, "No problem." What he did not know was that my heart had just dropped into the bottom of my stomach and was beating very fast.

    I smoke weed daily and now he wants me to take a drug test that I am guaranteed to fail. There is nothing that I will be able to do to my body that would cleanse me of THC in the next hour because I am saturated with it. Think, think, and think… who you can call with clean piss. The downside of smoking marijuana is that all of your friends smoke also so you can't really call them for help in this situation. What am I going to do? I have to get this job, let me figure out who to call. I called one of my friends that I went to high school with and was living in the same city. Ring, Ring…… ring…... Hi you have reached Toya, I am not home now….." Shit!!!!!! Who else can I call? Oh, wait, let me call Belinda. Ring….... ring…., "Hello." "Belinda, girl thank God you answered the phone. I need a big favor girl!!! "Belinda replied, "What's going on?" "Girl, I just had a job interview, and everything went well but now they want me to take a drug test. Girl you already know my situation. Can I bother you for some clean pee?" Belinda fell out laughing. I said, "I know girl, this is funny, but I really need you." Belinda said, "Girl I got you, come on over and I will start drinking some water now." I said, "Thank you, thank you, thank you!!! I love you!!" Laughing, Belinda hung up the phone.

I headed right over to her house and she opened the door. I walked in, apologizing for such short notice. She said, "Girl, you are fine. You have to do what you have to do. After coming from the bathroom, she handed me a zip loc bag with urine in it. I stored it safely on my person and went to the testing site to get this over with. Once, at the testing center, I went in and filled out the paperwork. I sat down and waited for my name to be called. I was as nervous as a child hiding something from their parent and praying that momma doesn't find out. "Stephanie." I responded, "Yes." "We are ready for you," said the attendant at the testing center.

I walked to the back and the attendant gave me instructions. She said, "Go in the bathroom, pee in this cup and fill it up to this line. Do not flush when you are finished. Do not turn on the water or do anything after you have given the cup back. Do you have any questions?" I said, "No" I looked calm and cool on the outside, but on the inside I was freaking out. I kept taking breaths, trying to get it together because I could not risk getting caught. I was shaking and my heart was speeding. It was beating so fast I could hear my heartbeat out of my chest. This was nerve-wracking, but there was no stopping me now.. It was now or never. I went into the bathroom. Thank God for those vents that make noise while someone is in the bathroom because that helped to ease me. I was so afraid of someone hearing me take out the bag to pour it into the cup. I squatted over the toilet while I did this so the attendant could hear leftover pee going into the toilet. Finally, the clean pee was in the cup and my pee was in the toilet. I put the zip loc bag back in the place where I had stored it. I didn't want to risk leaving it there in the garbage and someone figuring out what I had done. All evidence goes with me.

Okay I was ready to come out of the bathroom. I handed the attendant the cup with the clean urine and asked if I could now wash my hands. After I finished washing my hands, I asked if there was anything else that I needed to do. The attendant informed me that I was finished, and I could go. I walked out feeling refreshed and at ease with the contentment of a mission accomplished. Once in the car, I lit a cigarette and smoked that thing like it was the last one I would ever have in my life.

A few days later I got the call that I had gotten the job and would be working the overnight shift. I was happy and not happy at the same time. Of course, I was grateful and blessed for having a job. Damn, I have to work during the overnight shift during the nights that I like to go out and party. That sucks, but I needed work and I was going to do what I had to do, by any means necessary. Especially after what I had just done to get the job. Oh, I was going to work there until they kicked me out, or I found something better.

The house we lived in with our friends was the party house. We had all the party favors that anyone could want, except for Yoda; but we didn't indulge too much with that. When the weekends came, it was time to party and turn up. I would usually be excited when the weekend came but I usually had to work. I didn't mind working because a paycheck came with that, so I could not complain too much. This left my husband to hang out with my friends when it was time to party, which I also didn't mind too much, but I wanted to party with them. Not only was this free time for my hubby to hang out with my friends, but it also provided ample time for the hubby to get to know Maria better. I wasn't really on edge or anything. My other friends were around, but I wasn't there to observe, and that made me somewhat uncomfortable.

When I moved back to Gainesville, I was in touch in Shawn. He had moved to the mid-west but kept in touch with me to keep up with Eric and me. I talked to Shawn every now and then, so I'd have a male to talk to also about Eric. Especially because

Shawn knew Eric and could give his honest opinion about my concerns. A few months into moving in with my friends, Shawn had called and spoke to my home girl, Claudia. He asked her if he could move in temporarily until he got situated. Shawn was also trying to find his way in this world, like many of us living in that house. It was the party house, there was never any real privacy, but it was much better than being somewhere you did not want to be. Shawn showed up at the house one day and I was shocked. I didn't know that he was really planning on coming. Shawn's mom had died some months prior and he was living with his sister at the time. I guess he was ready for a change, or at least to be able to enjoy the freedoms that we all used to enjoy together back in the day.

Upon Shawn's arrival, I was happy to see him, but I instantly became a little uneasy. No one could tell, but on the inside I was battling with myself. I was married to Eric now, but I still had unresolved emotional attachment to Shawn. When Shawn and I were seeing each other in college, it was purely a casual sex set up. I liked him more than just having casual sex, but never wanted to say anything to push him away because I liked him. I felt that being in his life in the way that we interacted with each other was better than not being in his life at all. I guess I did not think highly enough of myself to say what I wanted and if I didn't get what I wanted, then to end the affair. When Shawn and I stopped seeing each other it was because I felt that he had someone else that he was seeing and was moving more toward a relationship with her; and one thing about me is I will run fast to avoid being hurt. So instead of him calling it off eventually, I just stopped calling and contacting him for sexual reasons. We were still friends and still saw each other out in public, but that was it. I had moved on to someone else.

Now that Shawn was living in the house with all the rest of us, I could not help but have some concerns. This was a 3-bedroom townhouse that had a little yard and a patio, but it wasn't huge. My friend Claudia had a room to herself and the other room was occupied by the 2 small kids that lived in the house at the time. The third room is where Eric and I slept. My friend Ken had gone to jail for a while. He was a repeat offender. Every few years he would go to jail and spend a few years there. Then he would get out, start his life over somewhat, get in a decent position and for one reason or another, get locked up again. That was his life. We were definitely thugging it out. We didn't have a bed, so I pulled the pillows from the couch to sleep on the floor. There were also some blankets being used along with a few pillows. This is where my concern became elevated. Shawn was to sleep in the room with Eric and me. Since we were all roommates before, we should be comfortable sharing a room. This might have been comfortable for them, but for me, this was a major test. I knew that Eric and I had an open relationship, but this was the ultimate test of loyalty. I was not in a happy place, but I couldn't really talk to anyone about my feelings. The only person I could talk to was Claudia and she might have said something, so my best bet was to keep my thoughts to myself at this time.

So, one night we were all lying in the room to go to sleep for the night. Naturally, because there were two guys and a girl, and we still had no bed, I slept in the middle of the two of them. It was like when we were all roommates all over again. The problem was, now I am married to one of them and this could get messy. Shawn wasted no time making his move. I made sure to lay up under Eric as closely as possible with Shawn being far away. It didn't take long for Shawn to make his move once he felt that we were both sleeping. I had my body hugging against Eric and one leg straddling his back because he slept with his back to me. He slept on his side and he was facing opposite of the direction that I was in. I didn't know if Eric was asleep or not, but I did my best to make sure that he knew any and everything that was going on.

Shawn began rubbing his hand straight to my vagina. I moved his hand and said stop. He went for it again, and again I said stop and pushed his hand away. This went on for minutes, but Shawn was the type of guy that felt like persistence would get him what he wanted. My mind was saying no, but my body was saying yes. I think he could feel the sexual energy coming from my body. See the issue for me was that I was still attracted to Shawn and could not act on that attraction because I was now married to Eric. Plus, Shawn was not going to make it easy for me to resist him. After several tries, Shawn did make way through to my loveliness and was able to penetrate with his finger. I was lost in the moment and then I realized what was going on and pushed him away and said to please stop.

He left me alone that night after that, but it certainly wasn't the last time that he came for me and I knew it would not be. I felt like he knew that I was still attracted to him and he was going to use that to his advantage. Oh my goodness, what is this that I am in the middle of? I wondered if Eric could tell what had happened, or if he was even awake. Oh I want to scream. I don't know what to do, but I don't like this set-up. Well it didn't take long for the next occurrence. This time it was a night we were all rolling, and Shawn cornered me. I was coming out of the bathroom from taking a shower. Wrapped in a towel with my bath caboodle in hand, Shawn walked in and would not give me room to walk out of the bathroom. I backed up asking him to move please. He said, "Why do you want me to move?" I said, "You know why." As we were talking, there was underlying flirting going on. By this time, Eric had not come home from work yet and this was a night that I did not have to work. Shawn and I were now alone in the bathroom and he made sure to lock to door behind him, once the door was closed.

My heartbeat started going at 100 beats a second. On one hand, I really did get turned on when Shawn and I were in close proximity; but at the same time we would be wrong for pursuing anything. Even though Eric said at the beginning of our relationship that he wanted to have an open relationship because he didn't want us to ever break up because of cheating, this still didn't feel right. I think that was also a part of the attraction. The fact that it may or may not have been okay, but deep down knowing that this probably should not move any further is what made the situation even more of a turn on. Indulging in something that you are not supposed to have is about the risk-taking.

Now Shawn had me pinned up against the sink in nothing but a towel wrapped around me and a caboodle in my hand. He started kissing me and I immediately pushed him away. He said,

"My bad, I thought that's what you wanted me to do." My response was, "What would make you think that I want that when I am married now? I do have some attraction to you, but we cannot act on that because this just isn't right and we just got married some months ago." As I finished my statement, Shawn went in for another kiss and this time it made my body melt. I was so weak to those of the male species, especially when there was an attraction. As he kissed me, I dropped my caboodle kit on the floor and did what I could to keep my towel from falling. Of course, his hands began to wander as he was kissing me and this time

I let him kiss me. Who was I kidding, I wanted it and sadly he showed me more attention sexually than Eric did. Remember, my reason for wanting to get married was to get Eric to pay more attention to me. I wanted Eric to want me and show that he wanted me, but that was always an area that we had problems with as a couple. Shawn was now fondling me while he kissed me on my lips, neck, ear and other parts above my neck. However, his hands were below the belt. He fondled my breasts then went directly for my happy place. It was already a little moist by what was happening. Shawn picked me up and sat my body up on the sink that was connected to the countertop. Once my body was secure on the sink he tossed my legs up above his head and I gripped the sides of the countertop to hold on. Shawn put his head down in between my thighs and licked his tongue out and rubbed it around on my clitoris. He then began sucking on my kitty kat and it felt so good. I closed my eyes and dreamed. I knew that what we were doing wasn't necessarily the right thing to do, but my body was so overdue for some good head.

The sex with Eric was okay, but he definitely needed help in the oral sex department. I would tell him what I liked, but it just wasn't that great for me a lot of times. I'd rather get on top and ride Eric until he came. While Shawn was sucking on my vagina. He had this gap in the front of his teeth. When he sucked on me he would pull my clit into the gap while playing with me. That drove me crazy. I grabbed his head and pushed it further into me so that I could get the full effect of what he was doing. This went on for few minutes before I whispered, "You know we can't go any further than this point right?" as I moaned, I talked at the same time. With his mouth on my vagina, he said "yes" and nodded his head. I said, "Cool, I just want to make sure that we are on the same page." I let him finish what he was doing. While I had a hold of his head I was moving my body around with his motions to make sure to get the maximum effect of this head session. I moved my clit back and forth in and out of his teeth which made me extra sensitive. I started to feel that excitement that let me know it was about to happen and that made me move faster until I let out a moan that was soft yet firm while I gripped his head for a few seconds. This is what happened when I bust a nut as the guys would say.

I was breathing hard. I wanted to take this further so badly but knew that I could not. But a nice firm hard and thick penis is all I needed after that great head session. He stood there smiling at me. Like he knew I wanted the D, but I had to stop it there. After I climaxed I told him to leave the bathroom please. I got back into the shower and took another bath to wash away my sins. I felt bad, but not bad enough to regret it. I needed some good pleasing. Shortly after returning to the shower for the second time, there was a knock at the bathroom door. I said, "Who is it?" The voice responded, "Baby it's me. I just got home from work." I said, "Oh, Ok, come in." Eric walked in the bathroom. I said, "How was your day?" he replied that it was fine and that he brought some food home for us if I was hungry. I told him that I would come and eat once I finished in the shower and he said okay and left the bathroom. In my thoughts I was feeling like I should say something to him about Shawn, but he did say we could have an open relationship. I just didn't want to cause any problems because we all lived together now. I thought about and decided to keep this tidbit to myself. Damn that session with Shawn felt so good. Why did I rush into getting married? This was my life now and I had to do the right thing. This sucks. My freedom is gone.

Now I see why Eric was hesitant about getting married. I could never tell him this and get the "I told you so" look from him. He could never know that he might have been right about marriage because that ultimately would mean we were not ideally the best match for a couple. After I finished in the shower, after my long conversation with myself, I went in the room and got dressed, and then went out into the rest of the house with everyone else. I tried to eat a little something, but I didn't really have an appetite because I had already popped a bean. That night we rolled and drank and smoked and that was that.

Eric's birthday was during the spring in April. Since there were a lot of people in the house, I wanted to surprise Eric. I got a room at a hotel that had a Jacuzzi tub for a weekend for the two of us. I wanted to make a weekend of it, and I wanted to do it so that we could have some alone time. I had a plan and everything. I would have one of our friends pick him up from work and bring him directly to the hotel from work. She would act like she had to stop there for something and ask Eric to come up with her and when they walked in I would be waiting for Eric in one of those sexy outfits. I went and bought some candles and strawberries and chocolate and some other things to make it a sexy night. He had been working hard and he deserved a nice night to just relax and let go.

So the night arrived, and I was at the room waiting for him and my friend to arrive. I was a little nervous. Wondering if he would like the surprise or if he would be surprised at all. Would he like the way I looked in the outfit? A lot of thoughts started going through my mind. I began to have doubts and I began to overthink and overanalyze like I tend to do when my mind wanders. Then I heard a knock at the door. It was them. I opened the door and my girlfriend walked in first, then Eric came in behind her. They were walking in hesitantly. I smiled at him. I said, "Do you like it baby?" and looked around the room and asked if anyone else was there. I said, "No, why do you ask?" He replied n a tone of worry, "When we pulled up and I saw the car I thought you were here seeing some man." My friend responded, "that was my bad when we came earlier you were parked on the other side so when I came back I parked on this side not realizing that I was parking right next to your car."

I gave her that look of, you almost ruined my surprise; but thank you and I appreciate you at the same time, while smiling. I walked over to Eric and gave him a hug and kiss and said, "Happy birthday." I went over to the countertop and grabbed some party favors, a rolled up blunt, and made a drink for the two of us and walked back over to Eric said, "do you want to light it, or do you want me to do it?" While this was going down my friend looked at me and said, "I think that's my cue." Eric said, "Before you spark that, let me run by the house and grab some clothes for the weekend." I pulled out a bag that I packed for him before I left the house. Some clothes, some toys that we liked to use when we were having relations among other things. Eric smiled and said, "Baby, you were thinking of me." as he kept smiling. "Baby, I am always thinking about you I have all of your favorites and me of course. Your weekend is straight."

My girlfriend responded with, "Well, like I said, that's my cue, I'm out. Let me know if you need anything." We all laughed, and she was gone. Eric went to take a shower and found a bubble bath waiting for him. I made sure to make it warm but not hot like I like it because I wanted it to be comfortable for him. There were candles along the side of the tub with slow jams playing on the radio that I put in the bathroom for ambience. We had the smell-good candles too. None of that cheap stuff. There was a dimmer in the bathroom, so it was slightly lit, but not too much. There were also rose petals floating on top of the bubbles in the tub. It was a very romantic scene.

Upon entering the bathroom, Eric had a surprised look on his face and also a look of relief. I guess it was because he thought I was at the hotel seeing some dude. I can't believe that he actually thought I was at the hotel visiting someone else. Especially with the other issues in my life. My intentions were good, but life throws some curveballs at you sometimes and it is the decisions that are made that dictate how your future will be. I began undressing Eric and preparing for him to get into the bath. Once in the bath, I lit the blunt and grabbed an ashtray and joined him in the water. Eric and I had already popped our beans prior to getting in the tub so we were in relax mode, smoking and allowing our beans to kick in.

As we began to feel good, and it was obvious when that happened, we both began rubbing on each other's body parts. Legs, thighs, privates, upper body, just all over, pretty much. We relaxed in the tub for a while. After we finished smoking, I got out to grab our drinks from the other room. I came back and got into the water. This time I began playing with him in a sexual yet playful manner. We finished up in the tub and went into the room. Now for the real fun to start. The beans had kicked in and we had been sipping and smoking, so we were feeling good. I told him to give me a minute. I went in the bathroom and put on one of the outfits that I brought. It was a cute lil number. It had a white shirt that tied up in the front to make my boobs sit up and showed off my belly. It came with a very short plaid tennis skirt. I put on the necktie that came with and some black stiletto heels along with fishnet thigh highs for the effect. After I dressed, I sprayed myself with a light smell-good to make me irresistible to any man, but especially to this man that I called my husband.

He was so picky at times. I was a little nervous, but that went away quickly. That's why I loved ecstasy so much. Those feelings of insecurity and uncertainty were gone when I was rolling. I walked out of the bathroom and Eric said, "Damn! Look at you" with a huge smile on his face. "Do you like it? I tried to find something I thought you would enjoy." Eric replied, "Yes, Absolutely, I really like it, a lot!" His eyes were big as his smile. I sashayed over to his side of the bed and kissed him, making sure to bend over so that he could see this entire ass that I had to offer, especially in this scantily clad outfit. As we kissed, he grabbed my ass and smacked it a couple of times as well. Something about when he smacked it made my lady parts tingle. While we kissed he grabbed on my breasts and fondled them with one hand while the other hand slid past my ass and between my thighs. I knew where he was headed, so I made sure to open up the space between my thighs so that his fingers could roam. The anticipation was a turn on as well.

As his fingers roamed they found my happy place covered with the black lace thongs that were between his fingers and my love hole. His fingers began to rub the outside of the thongs and they instantly became moist. This turned me on so much that I stopped kissing him and moved down to his chest and began to lick and suck on his nipples while I moved my hand up and down his male gender. I felt it growing in my hand while I paid it attention. I moved my mouth down to his male part and put the entire penis in my mouth and slowly moved my mouth down until the tip of his penis hit the back of my throat. While it was at the back of my throat, I began to hum so that he could feel the vibration of my mouth. He moaned and I knew that I was doing something right.

I liked to tease him sometimes, so after I did that I stopped and jumped up and said, "Wait!" with excitement. I grabbed the bag that I packed with our goodies. I pulled out a blindfold and some handcuffs. The soft kind of handcuffs that didn't hurt. I placed the blindfold over his eyes. He said, "What are you doing?" I told him to relax and lay back. I placed the handcuffs on his wrists and tied him up to the bed. He said, "Baby, what is going on?" I said, "Let me do this," while I smiled with a sexy smirk. After he was securely tied to the bed with the blindfold on, I pulled out a boa that was made of feathers. With R. Kelly's

12-Play playing in the background, I felt really sexy and silly. I started at the bottom of his legs and slowly moved the feathers up his body in a real sensual manner. Moving up his thigh, I slowly moved the feathers around the thigh next to his penis but never touching it. I moved to the other leg and worked my way up. Doing the same thing on that side of his penis. I climbed on top of him so the feathers could move about his chest. I placed one of my breasts in his mouth so that he could use his tongue to please my nipple while I moved the feathers around his upper body very slowly. I could tell that it was getting to him from the way that his body responded to the gestures. I switched and placed my other breast in his mouth taking out and putting it back in to mess with him. He could only use his lips and tongue, so this was fun for me.

After maneuvering around his body with the boa, I got the edible warming lube. It warmed up to friction. I put some lube on the tip of his penis and used my lips to give it some friction. Then I blew on the tip of his penis so that it would warm up. As the lube dripped down his shaft I blew on it with my lips barely touching it so that he could feel the warmth from it. He definitely seemed to like this because his body started squirming. I liked to make him squirm and he had no control. I was in control of everything and I loved it. "Damn, why are you messing with me like this?" he said in a flirty voice. "We are just having fun aren't we?" I moved my mouth down and licked on his balls before I put them both in my mouth. It's so funny because there was a time in my life that I said I would never put a penis in my mouth. My girlfriends would laugh and say that they'd bet that I would enjoy it if I did it.

It took a long time in my adulthood before I actually performed oral sex on my significant other. The first time it was different, but it took a few times for me to get comfortable doing it. Once I got comfortable, I noticed my lady parts would tingle when I did it and it started to turn me on when I did it. That made me want to do it more because at that point I actually started liking it. Along, with the fact that my mind was in the gutter 75% of the time, that just added to the fantasies that I had in my head. *Is that bad?* I liked sex and sexual things so much that they consumed my thinking most of the time, even since I was younger, before I actually had sex for the first time.

Now I had his balls in my mouth and was moving my hand up and down his shaft. I grabbed the boa and slowly moved it up and down his thighs, while teasing him up and down his shaft. Looking at his face this was a lot for him to handle because he looked like he was trying to keep it together. After a few moments of intertwining the use of the boa with playing with his manhood and licking and sucking on his chest he exploded out of nowhere. Creamy white lava shooting up and out and all over everything in the vicinity. I laughed because this was definitely something new that I tried and apparently it worked. He laid there looking exhausted.

My work here was done. We enjoyed each other for the rest of the weekend. We reconnected and that was a good thing. We had endured so much stress on our relationship since being married. It felt good to really have fun with each other like we used to.

CHAPTER SIX

Eventually we moved out of the townhouse that we were living in. Eric called that old place the "Den of Iniquity". Probably because it was the party house and there was so much that could threaten our relationship in that house. The many people in and out and the drugs and alcohol. Not that he didn't partake in them, but he judged the rest of us for our actions in participating. In the new house, there were four bedrooms. Eric and I had the master bedroom, Claudia had a room and her daughter had a room.

Shawn also had a room in this house. I was so not on board with him moving with us, but I couldn't really express why; and when it all came down to it, I was outnumbered in the vote to allow him to have that fourth room. I truly wanted to move on with no drama in my life, but I knew that it would not be so easy. With this new house, I had rules. We could have fun and party, but nothing was to be sold from this house. I wanted to have a fresh start. The weekend parties continued. There was not as much traffic. We did have friends that came by and hung out, but it was a little more reserved.

Eric and I were in a better place in our relationship. During those weekend parties, we rolled all night and when the sun started to come up, I went to sleep. Many of those nights, Eric would stay up for days. I needed my beauty rest. Eric would just hang out with whoever was still in the house. Maria used to frequent our house, which I didn't mind as she and I had our own friendship and I was more comfortable with her being around. I did have issues at first because when she came around, all of the men in the house would just fawn all over her, even Eric. I had to straighten him out a few times and remind him that I was his wife, not his girlfriend.

What I didn't know was that Eric and Maria were getting closer; especially those nights where I would fall asleep and he would stay up popping more beans. I came to understand that Eric had an addictive personality. I could take a couple beans and be fine for the rest of the evening, but Eric just wanted to take more and more. I never paid attention to this until it was too late, and I was already in several years.

While Eric and Maria were getting closer, I had been approached by Shawn in the new house. I truly tried my best to not want him and to not be attracted to him, but my body responded when he came near me and I had no control over my own body's feelings. This was so confusing. I would avoid him if he happened to be in the common parts of the house alone. If other people were around he acted like it was all good, but when no one was there, he was coming directly for me. This was so hard. After many times of getting him to stop what he was trying to start, I got weak. Eric and I only had one car, so many times during the weekend I would have to drop him off at work. I usually would go back home and get back in the bed because it was the weekend and I worked so hard during the week, plus I was usually recovering from the night before. I was a very hard worker and good at whatever it was that I did at the time. At times, I was left home alone with Shawn, depending on everyone's schedules. Let's just say it was a struggle each time.

Shawn was no better. I was beating myself up on the inside because of feelings that I was having for this man living in the same home, but it seemed that he was not concerned that Eric and I were married or that he and Eric were friends prior to me meeting either of them. This one particular morning, I got home and went back to bed after dropping Eric off at work. I was fast asleep upon falling into the plushness of the pillows and comforter that lay on the bed. While I was sleeping, I awakened to a hand slowly moving up the inside of my thigh. My first thought was, "Damn, I should have locked the door!" Upon opening my eyes, I see Shawn standing over me on the side of the bed that I sleep in with Eric every night. I rolled over to make his hand move and acted like I didn't even see him. Again, my mind was saying no, but my body was saying yes. *Now I see what R. Kelly was talking about.* How much I wanted to not do something that would negatively affect my marriage, but damn my juices were starting to flow. After rolling over, as to ignore Shawn, he grabbed my legs and turned them in the direction that he was in and spread them open wide and began to indulge in breakfast with what was between my legs. I couldn't stop him. I really didn't want to stop him. I liked it. A lot!!! I wanted him to do what he was doing; but in actuality, it should not have been happening.

When my mind goes from the pleasure of it to the possible consequence of this action, I am now in a mode of "this can't happen." I told him to stop, but he kept going and I kept liking it. My body told my mind to stop fighting it and just let it happen. I stopped trying to push him away and gave in because I really did want it, even though I wasn't supposed to. That was the beginning of what should not have happened but did. We had hard passionate sex. The kind you know you had better enjoy because it may never happen again type of sex. The kind that you know you will be fantasizing about later on and in the near future.

When we released each other after it was all over, it's like we both knew we had a problem.

There was so much emotion pinned up inside of us that this release of energy came right on time. Not in the best of ways, but Damn! I vowed to myself after that session that Shawn and I would not engage in anymore sexual activity, but it happened a few more times after that. It kept happening, until I started locking doors. I wasn't safe in my own home. I mean I wasn't going to be harmed, but I can't just be available. Anything was liable to happen.

Maria and Eric were becoming the best of friends. Unbeknown to me at the time, Eric and Maria were spending a lot more alone time together when I would be at work or when I was sleeping. Maria would frequent the house like certain other friends. Maria would hang out with my roommate Claudia when we all partied and during the non-partying time as well. At first, I didn't think much of their relationship. I wanted to give him space and allow him to have friends and things of that nature. I knew they had the same birthday, so they had a lot in common.

Eric and I had somewhat conflicting schedules. I worked Monday thru Friday 8am until 5pm. Eric worked at a restaurant, so he worked more weekends and evenings. This caused a rift in the relationship. We did not have time for each other, but we had time for others. We began to have more arguments about everything. Over the time, our relationship had taken a wrong turn. We argued over not having time to spend together, excessive drug use, and not having sex. There were others, but those are the main issues.

I felt like being married was a mistake that we should not have jumped into so fast. I would tell him that. I am so quick to break up with a boyfriend when they piss me off and now I am married and cannot leave. I come from the type of family that stayed married, no matter what. Well, at least my grandparents did. I expected that when I got married, that would be it. That we were going to last until death do us part. I felt that I owed God to try to stay in this relationship for as long as I can because I have always been quick to up and leave a relationship when it was not going my way.

Our arguments got worse and worse over time. In the middle of one of them in particular, Eric blurted out, "Are you sleeping with Shawn?" I paused and said, "No! Why would you ask me that? Are you sleeping with Maria?" "Just tell me if you and Shawn are sleeping together!" No Shawn and I are not sleeping together. He said, "Would you tell me if you were?" I really did not want to hurt Eric's feelings by coming clean about Shawn and me. If I told Eric what was going on he would be hurt, and I don't know what he would do. I told Eric, "Baby, I would tell you, but there is nothing going on." "You still didn't answer my question. Are you sleeping with Maria?" Eric responded, "No, Maria and I have not slept together." I said, "So why are you spending so much time together? Especially when I am not around."

Eric and I continued our discussion and he dropped the subject of Shawn. I also dropped the subject of Maria, at least for now. I was so relieved because my heart stopped for a split second when the question was initially asked. I tried my best to not have the look of shock on my face when he asked. I felt like a deer caught in the headlights, for real. But I kept it as cool as I could. Eric did not bring up Shawn anymore.

After that incident, Eric and I tried to do things to spend more time together. The only thing that brought us together was drugs. We could pop some ecstasy pills and have a nice, relaxing, sensual time with each other. That was usually how we got back on the right track with each other. We would roll and have sex and smoke and drink. We had our own type of therapy for each other. It took a few months, but we were over our hump of daily arguments. We were reconnecting with each other again... I had finally found the strength to stop having sex with Shawn. When Eric wasn't home I made sure to go chill with my roommate; and when no one was home except Shawn and me, I would lock my room door so that he could not come in.

Shawn took advantage. I began to finally realize that he cared nothing about me in that aspect and that this was just free vagina without the extras of being in a relationship. I still liked the sex with him, but I knew it had to stop. He knew how I felt and knew that I wanted him as badly as he wanted me. However, as adults, we are supposed to show restraint and make hard choices that we sometimes don't want to make. And it was all physical. So as Eric and I reconnected, I became more in love with him. I started to think to myself, *Why did I have sex with Shawn? I'm around here being all selfish and my man working hard to help take care of us.* (We both split bills and everything, but you know what I mean.) We were a team and the way that I had been acting was not promoting the team. Eric and I had popped some beans on a weekend, a few months after the argument where he confronted me about Shawn. We were chilling, being all in love again.

One thing about me is that I overthink and overanalyze everything to the point where I can drive myself crazy... with just my thoughts. I mean to the point where I am having a full-fledged conversation with myself. My momma used to say, "Ain't nothing wrong with talking to yourself as long as you don't answer." I guess I was real crazy because I would answer and co-sign. I confused myself; I didn't need anyone else to do that for me. Eric and I were in the tub together, just chilling. As I said, I was feeling all in love. Fantasizing in my head. Another reason why no one should make important decisions while intoxicated.

As I lay on Eric's chest. Just underneath his chin, but with my head above the water, I thought to myself that I should be honest with Eric about the past. These thoughts kept going and I could not get them out of my head. As I had this conversation with myself while we were in the tub, my body began to adjust to my thoughts. As I was thinking of telling Eric about Shawn and I having sex, my heart began to race uncontrollably. I took deep breaths to calm down. Eric asked me if I was okay. I said that I was fine, even though I really wasn't. I just laid there and thought to myself of whether or not to say what was on my mind.

As my mind wondered and imagined all of the possible outcomes of revealing the truth, my body was responding to the different thoughts. It was as if I was living each event that was going on in my head in real life and it affected my emotional state. In my mind, I knew that I made up my mind and things were over with Shawn and I was going to be a better wife. Why did I feel so bad if we had an open marriage and could do this according to what he requested when we started dating? I think that I felt bad because it was something that I was keeping from him and I had lied about it as well. All of this was going through my mind while I was in the tub with Eric.

Again, I was rolling at the time and my warning to all is to never make an important decision while intoxicated. I said, "Baby, you know I love you right?" He replied, "Of course, why do you ask?" I responded, "No reason." As I continued the conversation with myself in my head, I told myself to just tell him. I don't know why this was eating me up so bad. *Could it be that they were friends, or that we all lived together, or that I was keeping something from him…….ughhhhh this is so much.* I wish my thoughts would just be quiet. My thoughts just kept beating me up in the brain. Then I just blurted out of nowhere, "I had sex with Shawn!" it was killing me to not say anything and this is how I knew that I could never do this again. I never want to do anything to hurt him again.

When the words flew out of my mouth, I was still laying on his chest. He did not react initially; he just responded with, "Your heart is beating so very fast. Is that why your heart was racing earlier?" I said, "Yes" with a solemn look on my face. I was wondering why he wasn't upset. I then realized, we were rolling, and reactions tend to be different while on this party drug. Everything was all good until the beans wore off. I assured him that it would never happen again. I said, "I thought it was okay at first because of this open marriage thing and then it just felt wrong."

He asked, "How recent did this happen?" I became as quiet as a child trying to think of a lie to blurt out. "That's not important. Just know that it is over with him. I just thought that since the three of us did what we did back then that…" He cut me off, "No it's not okay!!" "You're the one that wanted this open relationship anyway. This wasn't my idea" … as I sat up off of his chest. "That doesn't give you a pass to screw your roommate." "Well, what does it give me a pass to do?" "It allows us to open up our bedroom to make it more interesting." I said, "When you said that you wanted an open relationship it was so that neither of us would break up with the other for cheating." This conversation went on while we got out of the tub.

All of a sudden our happy little romantic time had ended. As I dried off and moistened my skin with lotion, he began pacing while in our room. Here is the part that I did not mentally prepare myself for when I was having a full-fledged conversation in my head. "Why, why did you sleep with him???" I thought to myself, *We did a lot, but sleep was not one of them*. I knew I couldn't say this out loud. It really would not have gone well. But still there was no sleeping involved. I did not respond to him. I understand that he needed time to cool off. He was upset and I was the cause. I quietly put on something comfortable, yet cute and sexy, to try and get him in a good mood.

During this time, not only were we rolling, but there were others at the house, plus my home girl Claudia that lived with us. Thank God that Shawn happened to not be home at the time that everything was unraveling. Eric started with more questions, "Did he give you head? Did you give him head? How many times did y'all have sex?!!!!" I softly responded, "We didn't do it that many times, let's just gets past this. It's over and that chapter is closed."

"You didn't answer all of my questions," he replied. I tried not to answer any questions. Do I tell the truth? Tell him yes he gave me head and I liked it more than when you give me head. No!!! I can't say that, and I didn't want to lie some more, so I just didn't say anything. I let him blow off his steam. He talked and talked and talked. While he talked, my high slowly started to wear off. I thought of anything that I could to make him calm down. I knew we had some more beans, so I grabbed two and walked over to him with one in my hand and said, "Here baby, take one of these," as I put one of them in his mouth. I didn't want to take the chance of putting it in his hand, I needed him to take this and calm the hell down. He was starting to get on my nerves.

During his rant, I said, "If you want to break up with me, I understand. I am so sorry. I didn't mean to hurt you." it sounded so cliché as I said it, but I was sorry, and my word is bond. One thing about me was that it didn't take much for me to leave a relationship. Now that I was married, it was not as easy to just walk away. I was supposed to work on it and make it work. The pain that I saw in his face that night made me know that I would never do anything to hurt him like this again. As a matter of fact, I thought to myself, *from now on, if we have any more threesomes it will be with women. Preferably women that like men and women.* I felt that I needed to do what I could to make him happy since I had sex with Shawn and enjoyed it. I felt bad for actually enjoying it enough to want more but knowing I could not indulge. *What is wrong with me???* I decided that I owed it to him to have only females in our threesomes so he would not feel threatened.

After he popped the bean, he continued on with his rant and I sat there as I started to feel mine, so I knew his was starting to kick in… that calmed him down. I made us a drink and rolled a blunt and patted the space next to me so that he could get the hint to come sit next to me on the bed. I said, "I know this is hard, but we will get through this." I kept apologizing and assuring him that this would never happen again. He was still pissed. I told him that I knew he was hurt and if he wanted to, he could just hit me in the face and get it over with. That's how bad I felt. As if I needed him to do something bad to me in order to make him feel better and to make me not feel so horrible. As he became more relaxed from the bean, he calmed down more. He was still upset, but we were able to just talk, and we began to really listen to each other.

The night was turning into morning. Of course, we were still up from the ecstasy. There were still a few folks in the living room and hanging out in the back; and Shawn came home early that morning. Shortly after arriving at the house, once he got situated, he came to our room to say what's up. His was a usual routine. We were all pretty open and free in regard to privacy. We all would hang out together when we were rolling, so this was nothing new. The only thing that was different was that Eric had just recently been informed that Shawn had been having sex with his wife; and Eric was NOT a happy camper about this.

Shawn knocked on the door and asked if he could come in. By this time, Eric was already at the door. I couldn't move fast enough. Eric opened the door and punched Shawn directly in the face, as Shawn was walking inside the room. Shawn yelled, "Man what the hell is your problem?" Eric swung at him again, "You know what the hell my problem is, you been screwing my wife!" Shawn paused; his face had a look of shock as if he had no idea of how to respond. Just as he paused, he got caught by another punch that was thrown by Eric. Shawn replied, "Eric stop hitting Me," as he threw out a punch at Eric. "Let's talk about this, damn!" Eric replied, "We have nothing to talk about," as he swung another punch but this time hitting Shawn in the gut. "Ow" Shawn mumbled, "Let's discuss this like grownups," Shawn replied. Eric grabbed Shawn and swung him into the door of the room. Shawn grabbed Eric and pushed him as hard as he could to get him off of him. They were breaking things that were on the dresser and shelves.

Blood was getting all over everything that they touched. They were both bleeding from their face. This went back and forth for a few minutes. Shawn said, "You said y'all had an open marriage, I thought that what we were doing was accepted. Anyway, you know we already had been together. What is the big deal???" Fists kept on flying between them. Shawn would hit Eric, then Eric would return the hit. I was in the room while most of this went on, but I got in a corner and didn't move. If they weren't punching and pushing they were swinging at each other. They went from the bed to the floor; everything was everywhere, and I did my best to stay out of the way. I didn't want to get caught up in the middle of these two fighting, so I stayed out of the way. That is until Shawn started to get the best of Eric during the fight. It was obvious that Shawn didn't really want to hurt Eric; but Eric was relentless, so Shawn had to slow him down.

Shawn hit Eric with a one-two to the stomach, then cheek; and knocked Eric to the ground. I yelled, "Stop it! Just stop it!! This is over!!! Shawn let him be." Shawn yelled back, "He came at me first. I am just trying to protect myself. I am acting in self-defense." "I know, but just leave him alone. Please!! Just Go!!!" Eric lay on the floor, he was out cold for a moment and came to in obvious pain, but I think his ego was more broken than anything at this point. Shawn had already left by now. I reached down to try and help Eric, but he wasn't having that. He was pissed at me, he was pissed at Shawn, he was pissed with the world and I understood. I tried again, "Baby get up off the floor. Let me help you into the bed." He pushed me away as he replied, "No, just leave me alone."

I knew he was hurt but, I couldn't just leave him there. I grabbed the comforter off of the bed and a couple of pillows and lay on the floor next to Eric. I wrapped my arms around him. Happy that he did not push me away, I held him as tight as I could. I began to hum a song quietly and he eventually fell asleep. I lay there wondering what the hell to do now. I thought to myself that *Shawn is going to have to move. We must have peace in this house. We will not have peace if Shawn continues to live here. I am going to have to tell him that he must leave as soon as physically possible. I don't want any more fighting; no more drama. I just want peace and love.* Why is that so hard?

I have always coined the term that "I am a lover of love," I just want love around me and inside of me on a few different levels. I loved Eric and I didn't want him to be hurt. I didn't expect him to go at Shawn in that way. It was a shock to me. Honestly, it felt good for a brief moment that my man was fighting for me; that was until he started getting his ass kicked. I then thought, *well damn, I ended up with the wrong one. But it is what it is, and I am married to Eric, so I have to stick this out.*

A week or two after confessing my sins to Eric, he starts hitting me in my sleep with a pillow. These were not love taps. Eric was putting all of his force into the hits. I woke up to him swinging the pillow at me with all of his force. After coming to and realizing what was happening, I swung at Eric and told him to stop it. Eric stopped hitting me with the pillow. I laid my head back down and went back to sleep. This dude starts hitting me again with the pillow. I woke up swinging at him. This time I grabbed my pillow and started swinging at him. "Eric stop hitting me, what the hell is wrong with you? I am trying to sleep." He kept swinging the pillow at me while I was talking. I jumped out of the bed and threw my pillow at him and stated, "Leave me the hell alone. If you don't want to be in this relationship, then leave; but what you ain't finna do is keep hitting on me."

Eric stated, "I am just so upset about you and Shawn." In response I stated, "I know and understand, but that door was opened when you kept insisting that we have an open relationship." By now, I am standing next to the bed and he is on the other side of the bed. He came close enough to me so that he could start hitting me again with the pillow. Eric hit me with the pillow so hard that my body flew backwards. *This nigga is really trying to hurt me.*

I pushed him away from me and grabbed the closest thing that I could. It was a round porcelain dish that we used as an ashtray. After pushing him off me I took that porcelain dish and held it up as if to throw it. Eric looked at me and said, "You better not throw it." That pissed me off even more. I threw that porcelain dish with all of my might directly at him. He called himself trying to duck so that the dish would miss him. Oops, his timing was bad. The dish hit him in the mouth. Blood started to come from his mouth and lips. "I can't believe you threw it", Eric stated. "I told you to leave me alone. I am not your punching bag. We can end this relationship now. I don't have time for this shit. Eric then apologized for hitting me with the pillow and I apologized about his mouth and warned him to never hit me again.

Time had passed and Eric eventually got over the situation with Shawn and me. Shawn moved out shortly after the incident and we stayed at the house for a little while longer. Then we all parted ways. Eric and I moved into our own place, Claudia and her daughter moved back to their hometown. Shawn had already relocated, so we were in our own spaces. Eric and I now had more privacy and we could do more things and possibly get into more adventures. And get into more adventures is what we did. By now, I had met a few more people and there was one particular person that peaked my interest and I knew I had to introduce to Eric. I knew that he would see why I was so elated with her. She was very down-to-earth, and we got along very well. And to tell you the truth, I didn't click too well with most women because I saw phoniness and bullshit from a mile away and most females thought that I was mean when I spoke the truth about things.

This girl was different. We did not argue, and we could have an intelligent discussion and not agree, yet still be friends. There were times that I would mention her in conversations between Eric and me and he commented that he was going to have to meet her one day because he had never heard me say anything negative about her the entire time that we knew each other. What's interesting is that this is several years after we moved out of the house; and during that period, Eric and I had conceived a child who by now was still a baby. Interestingly enough, this girl was pregnant when I met her. Actually we were pregnant at the same time, but her baby was born 3 months before my bundle of joy arrived.

We met at work; she had just started there and sat with me one day to see how the job was done. It was called shadowing and I usually had new people to shadow me because I was so good at what I did at work; and all of those in positions higher than mine knew that I knew the policy and procedures like the back of my hand and no one could come for the great job that I was doing.

Anyway, back to my friend. Her name was Sara and Sara had a lot of good qualities and I loved her point of view. One day, she and I were talking, and I happened to mention what Eric and I did during our extracurricular time. I don't know why this peaked her interest, but it did. I forgot to mention that by now, Eric and I had graduated in our world of extracurricular activities. We were now; not only smoking weed, popping ecstasy pills, but now we were taking bumps. A little bit here and there… nothing major. It was well-deserved; we worked hard during the week and needed the time to relax and just enjoy life with no worries. Even if it was only for the night. As Sara and I were talking, I told her that I try not to do too much because I eventually want to let that go. I said to Sara, "I keep trying to suggest that we don't do the white girl on the weekends, but it is all around me and that makes it hard. Not only is the temptation there, but it is also readily available. I know too many people in the dope game. Not by choice, but really by chance. Well maybe some by choice but not all of them." She replied, "Well why don't you just stop cold turkey." I responded, "Because if Eric wants some, he will get it and if it is in the house, I am doing it.

What are you doing this evening?" I was asking so that I could invite her over. She replied, "Nothing much planned except for the same thing that I do every Friday night, which is take a bath, put on some pajamas, pour me some wine and watch movies until I pass out." She said this while she chuckled . I said, "Cool, you should come by so you can meet my husband. We will get a bottle and chill. Probably roll up a couple of blunts, nothing major. We just usually are on chill mode." Sara responded, "Sure, let me make sure that my son's father will get him for the night, and I can swing through for a little while." "Cool," I said with a smile on my face. Later that night Sara came by the house.

What I didn't know was that my friend Ken had recently gotten out of jail from one his many stays in the county. So since Ken came by the house, it was only right that we pull out some type of party favors. It is time for celebration. I haven't seen my friend in a long time. We made a call and got some of that white stuff. We put it on a plate, and we sat around taking bumps off the plate. Ken, Eric and I were talking and catching up with each other. Ken was originally my friend since I was 19 years old in college and we remained close after our school days were over. We had a lot of catching up to do. We talked and talked and talked and then we heard a knock at the door. We had the music playing in the background, so I didn't hear the knocking until the second attempt. Or at least what I thought was the second attempt.

I had forgotten that Sara had sent me a text message that she was on her way. I opened the door and we greeted each other, and I invited her in. "Hey girl, how ya doing?" I said as I gave her a hug and walked her over to the couch. I made her a drink and she joined the conversation. I introduced her to my friend Ken and to my husband Eric. I knew that Ken was in for a treat because I knew that he was going to love her. I was excited because her energy and her spirit were so positive, and she made me smile, and that was hard to do.

We all sat there talking, smoking, drinking, etc. we were just having a good time. During the conversations, Eric mentioned that one of our friends from college was living around the corner from us. We knew that Ken would like to see him because of how long he has been away. It was a friend we nicknamed Blaque because he was chocolate as hell. I called Blaque and told him to come to our house because we had a surprise.

When Blaque arrived at the house, I opened the door and he saw Ken sitting on the couch. Instantly Blaque was like, "my homie, when did you get out?" as he walked over to Ken and they had a man hug moment. Ken replied with how long since he had gotten out of jail and they had a short catching up moment. After Blaque and Ken had a moment we continued with our conversation. Blaque walked around to take a seat on the couch and noticed that we had a little bag going around. He said, "Since the homie is back home here is another one," as he threw another bag of Yoda on the table with the bag that was already being consumed.

At that moment, I looked at Sara and said, "Now do you see what I mean?" She just looked at me and laughed and I laughed with her. The guys were looking at us like we had some issues because Sara and I had our inside jokes, but the fact of the matter was that I could not leave that life alone because I was attached to it in so many ways. I figured I might as well enjoy it because it is what it is. We had a great night, and everyone enjoyed themselves.

The next day Ken called me and left a message on my voicemail that I will never forget. He was so elated with Sara that he let me know the next day that he wanted to be in her aura and in the vicinity of Ms. Sara Honey. He sounded so in love; it was so cute. From the way that he sounded on the phone, she had all of a sudden become his everything and she was totally unaware. Ken was really feeling Miss Sara Honey. This was cute. They both had those types of spirits that are always positive and with good energy. I talked to Sara at work one day and informed her of what had transpired during the conversation with Ken and me. "Girl, I need to talk to you. Let me know when you go on break so we can talk." Sara responded, "Sure, no problem, we can go now." "Cool, I will meet you downstairs in the back," I responded.

The place that I worked at during that period was alright. The building had this little pond behind it where people would go walking or eat their lunch or just chill and talk during their downtime. We met back there and started talking. So I proceeded to tell her about how my friend, Ken, was just overjoyed with meeting Sara. I said, "So honey, let me give you the tea boo!! My homeboy that was at the house Friday when you came by, the one that just got out of jail, you remember who I'm talking about?" She replied "Yes, I do, he was cool." She responded. I continued," He is in love with your ass already. He called me like, please put me in the vicinity of Sara because I really want to be a part of her world. Please give her my number and ask her to call me." Sara and I laughed as I told her about Ken, and we continued talking. She asked me about whom he is and what he is about. I was honest. I told her how I knew him and explained that he is good people, but his decision-making skills are not the best.

Ken was the type of person that anyone would have a good time with. He is fun and spontaneous, but in regards to planning for the future, he is not the type of person that you can count on in that regard because you never know when he is going back to jail; and the decisions that he made in the past let me know that I cannot place all of my trust in him. I went to tell Sara that I knew early in our friendship that we could never be in a relationship, other than friends, because I knew him too well.

Sara and I continued to talk, and I gave her my honest opinion. I told her to at least give him a try and have fun, but don't put too much into a long-term relationship because it may not end that way and I didn't want Sara to get hurt. Some people call me mean, but the thing about me is I don't beat around the bush and I am honest, even if that honesty is brutal at times. Sara said she would give it a try. I gave her the number and we went back upstairs because we were well over our break.

Sara and Ken started seeing each other and they made a cute couple. Sara had moved to the town for school and now she was finished with school. We worked together for over a year, but when she was finished with school it was time for her to make moves. Sara eventually moved back to her hometown, but she and Ken continued to date. Ken sent for Sarah to come back into town and visit for a weekend. They had gotten very comfortable with each other and one night we were all hanging out. Of course when there were special occasions, the party favors were on deck.

We had green, beans, Yoda. It was really a party now. So we were doing what we did, we had music on, and we watched music videos while we talked, danced, smoked, did anything that we wanted because we could. A song came on that I liked so I got up and started dancing. While I was dancing, Sara came and started dancing with me in a very sexual manner. I was into it, so I let it happen. This was the first time that she had really gotten into my personal space like this. I mean don't get me wrong , we were cool, and I have told her about my past escapades, so maybe she felt like it was okay because I am an open and free-spirited woman. I was like, "Ok." While we danced together she began to get touchy feely and began to feel me up... I will admit I did like it, but I was a little confused. I like to have fun, but I don't like to mix business with pleasure. What I meant by this was that I considered her a friend and I didn't want us to go too far in a sexual manner and things go downhill and we are no longer friends. I had to think about what was happening, which was messing up my good time because I was overthinking everything that she did at this point.

While she got flirty with me, the guys just watched. Neither of them tried to stop Sara or myself, so I allowed it to continue. It felt good; I just had mixed feelings on what was happening and what could possibly happen past this point. As we danced, and Sara felt me up, moving from my ass up to my breasts, I was a little turned on but trying to keep my composure. We were supposed to be just chilling, how did we get here? I had to change my thought process and just enjoy the moment. I had this problem with over thinking and overanalyzing every single thing to the T. As I was thinking all of these thoughts, I danced with a smile on my face and when I decided to let go of all of the thoughts, I just closed my eyes and danced. All of a sudden these soft lips kissed mine and my eyes popped open. My pretty friend Sara is smiling at me. I said, "What are you doing?" with a smile on my face. She responded, "What's wrong, are you not comfortable?" I responded, "I'm fine, I just want to make sure we are on the same page and you know what you are doing, because you are starting trouble right now!"

Still smiling, she responded, "I know, that is the purpose!" With a smirk on my face, "Alright!" As long as you know what you are doing." She replied, "I do, and I am absolutely fine with that." We continued to dance, but now in a more flirty way with each other. Eventually the guys joined in with the dancing. Eric behind me and Ken behind Sara with Sara and I still facing each other and feeling each other up and down. Sara kissed me again, but this time I joined in. The first one had me shook. I didn't know what to do. I didn't know if I was ready for this. Honestly, the women I dealt with were the females that I had okay relationships with, but not really close; just in case things didn't go well I would be fine with letting go of that relationship.

Sara was different. I enjoyed her company, and as a friend I was torn. But I continued anyway with kissing her and caressing her body parts as she had done mine. Eric was behind me grabbing whatever he could and same goes for Ken with Sara. It's almost as if the guys had to remind us girls that they were there. Sara and I were into each other as if no one else was in the room. Now everyone's hands were going all over the place. Eric was feeling up both Sara and me, Ken was also feeling up both of us ladies. My hands began to wander in Ken's direction and Sara's were in the direction of Eric and we all just explored each other for a while. There was kissing, caressing, licking, sucking and everything going on.

It got so intense for a moment I had to stop. I was getting very overwhelmed. I said, "Wait y'all, let's make sure this is what we want because this is moving in a direction that I wasn't ready for. I went and sat down on the couch. Sara sat next to me and the guys were on either side. I lit the blunt that was halfway smoked sitting in the ashtray. As I smoked I passed it to Sara, she hit the blunt and blew a shotgun into my mouth. Our lips were barely touching. Damnit, this turned me on too. What was wrong with me? I was horny as hell and was uncertain on whether or not to take it further. This was so unlike me. I was always down for the party. Finally, I relaxed and just let the night happen. Sara and I started kissing and one thing led to another. Next thing I know I was topless along with Sara and we were sucking and kissing on each other. Eric was kissing and sucking on my body parts and Sara's, and vice versa for Ken as well. It was one big party and I was enjoying it. Like a big ole orgy with two couples.

Eric and I had participated in one of these before, but this hasn't happened in a long while. We were now married and living in a totally different city. But it's all good, I'm going to roll with the punches. Gradually, clothing began to hit the floor and hands and fingers were inside of us girls. I just kept trying to relax and enjoy. The same rules applied. The guys would penetrate their own ladies but everything else was fair game. In the midst of everything Sara threw me down on the couch and began to suck on one breast while Ken sucked on the other and Eric was practicing his "giving head" skills. He was getting better.

I was being taken advantage of and I loved it. This was what really turned me on. The feeling of being wanted was more of a turn on than actually being touched. At least for me. It let me know that someone other than myself really deeply appreciated me for the person, woman, feline, sex kitten that I am. It allows for a closer connection than actual penetration. The person that it came from was even more overwhelming because of the fact that I loved and enjoyed her as a person; and now that we are here touching and kissing on each other like this has created a fantasy within a fantasy for me. The night went on and we all got more down and dirty. It was great. I was ecstatic. When it was said and done, the four of us laid on the floor in the living room on a comforter, catching our breath while rolling up a blunt. I was in heaven at this moment.

After that day had passed, Ken and Sarah continued to see each other for some months after our rendezvous. Then Sarah got a chance to find out what I meant about Ken and his decision-making skills, especially when it came down to planning for the future. She told Ken that she was opening a savings account for him. The only expectation was for him to send her a certain amount when he got paid so she could put it into his account for him. He started off okay with the first couple of months. After that, he stopped sending money for the account. I mean he would still spend money and buy her nice things, but he wasn't saving anything and that aggravated the hell out of Sara.

Eventually they broke up; yet remained friends. Ken was the kind of person you could not stay mad at because of his personality. He was so happy go lucky. Even when he knew he was going to jail, he did not have a care in the world. That's what I loved about him. Time went on and I had kept in touch with Sara, of course. We were friends and I liked her. We would talk every few days and I would update her on what was going on with me and others. I told her that I was planning a party for my birthday. I was not quite sure of the details just yet.

By this time Eric had stopped working and I was the only one bringing in some bacon. I made a decent amount because I had gotten a raise, then a promotion; so I was no longer living paycheck to paycheck. But with having to take care of the family, I had to really budget the finances to allow Eric and me to enjoy ourselves at times. I missed Sara and wanted to see her again. I thought to invite her to come down for my birthday. I had rented a room at a hotel that had a suite with a Jacuzzi tub. "Sara would you be able to come down for my birthday party?" I asked during one of our conversations. Sara replied, "Now girl, it is kind of tight for me. I am still adjusting to a new job and trying to buy myself a house. I don't think I will be able to afford a plane ticket." I asked, "How much do you think you would be able to afford?" She said, "I could probably put $100 towards it." I said, "Ok, let me look at flight prices and see if I can put in the difference to get you down here so we can hang out for my birthday…if that's cool with you." Sara responded, "Of course, I wouldn't pass up your birthday."

I could hear her smiling through the phone. I was excited already. We hung up the phone and I immediately went to searching for flights for the period of my birthday party. After an extensive search I found a decent price flight for a little over $200. I went ahead and booked the flight, then called and told her about the arrangements and details about her portion when she gets here. A couple of months had passed, and my birthday was coming upon us. I had already informed Eric of her arrival. I could tell that he was excited about her coming as well. For Eric and me it was always nice having a special friend, but she was very special. I think that we individually liked her as much as we liked each other, and we were married.

The time has arrived. Party favors, blunts, Patron and everything else to make a party a party was on deck. Eric even went out of his way to make a birthday cake for me which I thought was very special. I picked Sara up from the airport on the day before the party since she was staying for the weekend. Everything was going off without a hitch. We had the hotel room set up with balloons and streamers. Weed smoke was in the air, people were popping pills, drinking, getting a little freaky, dancing, and just having a good time. My job was done. I just wanted folks to come out and have a good time with no inhibitions and really just get it in… and that is exactly what we did.

By this time, Ken had already returned to jail again, for some odd reason. This never was a surprise. He usually went to jail for something drug-related because he always had them. If he didn't have them, he knew who had them. As the night progressed, I started to feel really good. I was rolling and I had been drinking. I wanted to get into the Jacuzzi, my favorite spot… especially when I have taken ecstasy.

I pulled Sara to the side and asked if she wanted to join me in the Jacuzzi tub. She responded with a yes. We went into the master bedroom where the Jacuzzi was and began to disrobe each other. We were smiling and laughing while we took off each other's clothing. I put bubbles in the water and made sure it was nice and warm while it was still running. I had a blunt rolled for us and we had our drinks next to the tub. We got in and just relaxed while we sat back and smoked the blunt. Sara and I were kissing each other as we smoked the blunt.

I guess Eric finally noticed that we had disappeared because not long after we had gotten into the tub, he showed up. By the time Eric showed up, the blunt was almost finished and we needed our drinks refreshed. "Eric, honey, can you pour us up a couple more cocktails, please?" I said to him, as I gave him my empty glass. Sara held her glass up as well to motion that she wanted another. "Sure baby, is there anything else that I can do for you while I'm up?" "No, we are good, thanks," I responded.

As soon as he walked out, Sara and I started making out in the tub. We were kissing and licking and sucking on each other. We were so engulfed in each other for the moments that we were alone that we didn't notice Eric standing watching us as we touched and caressed and explored each other's body. "Hmm…" Eric made a noise as if he was clearing his throat. Sara and I stopped to see where the noise came from before we realized it was him. "Can I join you?" I looked at Sara and said, "I don't know, can he join us?" "Sara smiled and said, "He sure can." Eric got into the tub and the three of us were in the tub making out with each other.

This time Sara was in the middle and we all made out with each other. Eric was fondling Sara. His fingers were entering holes that are only explored by the special kind. I was all over her breasts and she was all in mine. I had lit the blunt that Eric rolled while we were in the tub. As I inhaled, I blew the smoke into Sara's mouth and we began to kiss. I then inhaled and blew a shotgun into Eric's mouth. Eric and I began to kiss while I cupped Sara's breasts and he continued to fondle her. This tub rendezvous began to get steamy. We played with each other for a little longer while in the tub, then made our way to the bed. We locked the door and I lit some candles. I also put on some music to keep the mood going.

The three of us were in the bed and it was a very sensual experience. Lots of soft kisses and licking were being exchanged. I made my way to her lady parts and allowed my fingers to explore the atmosphere. Her moans let me know that she was enjoying this, so I continued. I began to kiss her softly on her thighs and around her belly button. She fingered Eric to come over to her. While I was inside her, she grabbed Eric's penis and began to go down on him. I could tell that this turned her on as well because I could feel her getting wetter the more she sucked on him. We were all having a good time. While she sucked on his penis, she whispered, "Tell it come here..." and I stopped what I was doing for a moment. I don't know why, but all of a sudden I was annoyed.

This was the first time she performed oral sex on Eric. I think I was a little jealous too because I never talked to his penis when I was giving him head and he really liked when she said that because his body jerked when she said it. Oh wow, was I jealous. Why did this upset me the way it did? I was confident in my relationship with Eric, but this little gesture somehow took me aback.

Was Sara now a threat to my relationship? We are just having fun. Sara could also tell that I hesitated because I stopped everything that I was doing at that moment. I didn't want to ruin our evening. We were having a great time. I continued and the night went on. We all continued to enjoy each other until we were exhausted. I didn't make mention of the feelings that I had about that night to either of them. I had to accept it because that is what we agreed to, upon entering into this type of relationship. If you want to be a big girl, you got to put on your big girl drawers and keep it moving. Therefore, I left the topic alone. I pretty much sucked it up. No pun intended.

The party was now over. It was the next day. We had checked out of the hotel and Sara wasn't leaving until Monday. We all chilled at our house just recuperated from the weekend, which was very eventful, mind you. We were smoking a blunt outside on the balcony while we sipped on our drinks. It was just Sara and me out on the balcony, chilling and talking about the past events and laughing. You know, just having girl talk. It was real chill. Then during our conversation Sara leaned over to me and said, "You seemed a little uncomfortable yesterday when we were, you know...." as she giggled. I replied, "I had already told myself that I was not going to bring it up because we were just having fun and I will get past that." Sara said, "If you don't want me to give him head anymore just say it because I don't want to make you feel uncomfortable or upset." "You know, I did feel some type of way because he liked what you said to him and I never do that. I am not telling you to stop, though. It was just different and if we are going to partake I have to get used to things happening that I may not be prepared for." In response Sara said, "No, if it's something you don't like, I won't do it." I said, "No it's all good and I appreciate that you feel strongly about protecting me. Thank you so much. This is why I like you so much. I am going to miss you when you leave." "I'm not gone yet," she responded. We both smiled and sat back and re - lit the blunt. It was really all good. I knew her intentions were good and that put me at ease. We kicked it with each other until she left the next day. That was a great birthday weekend. I wouldn't change it for the world.

Now back to reality. It was just Eric and me again. We had a few other female friends that we did things with, but no one was like Sara. My relationship with Eric was fine, but Eric had this way of not being considerate that I was his wife. For example, if we had recollections about past sexual events, he would make comments as if I weren't even in the room. We were talking about Sara and he made mention of how great he felt when she was giving him head and how it really turned him on when she said, "Tell it come here." I just looked at him. I said, "Ok, we get it, you liked it a lot. I mean damn, can you talk about something else?" He responded, "What's wrong with you?" I replied, "I don't want to continuously hear about how another woman made you feel so good, like I don't know what I am doing when I go down. Maybe I just won't do it anymore."

I rolled my eyes at Eric and focused my attention back on what I was doing before the conversation started. That was the first time that he mentioned that part of that night, but it wasn't the last. My husband now used this situation to piss me off during arguments or heated discussions. This showed me how much of an asshole he was. I never noticed that he liked to dig and poke at a situation, just to make me mad. Someone that loves a person would not do things to intentionally get them upset. I mean, of course, couples are going to not get along sometimes, but what I started to observe in Eric was that he wanted to intentionally hurt me, except he did it with his words. I never realized that he had this evil spirit in him. I didn't like it. These were the types of things that made me ask myself that million-dollar question….."Why the hell did I get married??????"

Time went on and we had a few more rendezvous with Sara because I liked her. It was so funny. We all decided to meet each other in Atlanta one weekend since it was a halfway point between where she lived and where we lived. We both had relatives there, as well. Although Eric pissed me off often, it didn't take much to get me back into a good mood. Once I knew we were going to see Sara, I was back into a good mood. So we were on the road. We arrived in Atlanta that evening and we pulled up to Sarah's sister's house. I was excited to see her. She was a good true friend and good person. I think that both Eric and I were happy to see her. It's like the two of us were better with each other in our relationship when she was around.

We got out of the car and exchanged hugs with each other. We said our hellos, and as we walked inside, we greeted everyone in the Livingroom area. It was Sara's sister, her sister's husband and another young man. I assumed he was a friend of the husband. Sara walked by me as we all said hello and then walked over to the unknown male and said this is my boyfriend Mark. I smiled and said hello and gave Mark a hug. I could play it off for a few seconds. Everyone introduced themselves and then we all sat down and had a drink. So Mark was Sara's friend from back home that she has known for a long time, but they recently started actually dating each other. I thought to myself, *that's nice, now the main person we came here to see was no longer just hanging out with us. Now she has a man. Was I in my feelings? She wasn't my girlfriend, but we had good fun together. Am I being selfish? I am only thinking of myself. She deserves happiness. She cannot just be out there waiting for when she would see us again.*

The type of relationship that we had was not made to last forever. It was made for fun. To be able to live in the moment, enjoy life. Not dwell on what the future might hold. I understand all of this rationality; but still I was not happy that she was now taken by someone else. "Hey y'all I'm going to step outside and have a smoke, I will be back. Eric, can you show me where the stuff is?" Eric looked at me like what are you talking about. I looked at him with piercing eyes and told him to follow me with my eyes. He said, "Oh let me show you where it is." Eric and I got outside where we were alone. As soon as I knew that the coast was clear I started going in…."Who the hell is this Negro she done brought down here with her? Is he supposed to be her man? Were we not enough? What about our relationship? Huh, What about that?" I was pacing back and forth while Eric lit a blunt.

I didn't want her to see my reaction because I had to play it cool, but I was not prepared for the newbie. She did not give us any warning or anything. I hit the blunt and was still pacing. Eric said, "Baby relax, it's her life, she can see whomever she wants." I replied, "I am fully aware that she has the right to see anybody on this earth that she chooses. I just wish she would have said something, that's all. Got me all excited to see her expecting one thing when obviously that is not happening; and I mean it is fine that it is not happening, but I got my hopes all up high like we were going to have fun like we did in the past, NOT! Like I said its fine, I just don't like to be blindsided. It's all good. It wasn't meant to last forever."

Eric is trying to change the energy by making me laugh. He said, "Sara got us here feeling like Mister and Celie when Shug Avery came into town with her new husband." We both laughed, and I had calmed down a little. I just kept hitting the blunt until

I could feel relaxed. Sara came outside alone and said, "Is everything okay? You seemed a little tense." I stated, "Naw, naw, I'm good. We good, there's no problem." In my mind, I was saying a whole lot, but I kept those comments to myself. "Yeah, we are good. We will be in shortly" After she felt reassured that we were good; she walked back into the house. Eric looked at me with those eyes, like… you need to get it together. I just smiled and let out a giggle. "Man this is some bull, but I'm alright. It is what it is." The blunt was almost finished. Eric and I laughed and giggled to each other about the entire situation and finished smoking so we could go back inside.

Sara and I remained friends, but our past rendezvous would be just that…in the past. From now on she belonged to another and I had to respect that. Eric and I laughed at that episode for weeks following. He was talking about, "We both with colds," while pretending to cough like Celie and Mister from The Color Purple. Eric did have a way of making me laugh, even though he got on my damn nerves sometimes.

CHAPTER SEVEN

People that know us always wonder why I go along with having an open marriage. I remember what Eric said to me when we began dating so many years prior. Having an open relationship would keep us from breaking up with each other due to the fact that is cheating. I understood that philosophy. If we left the doors of the relationship cracked with approval of the other we can still enjoy others and one another. This will allow each person to possibly enjoy someone else that they really want. Because if there is someone that you want to get it on with that strongly that you are willing to tell your partner about them then you might as well. It's funny though, because guys are so different. It is all good when it works in his favor, but if it doesn't he is ready for all hell to break loose. I also noticed that Eric was happier with our arrangement because I was only bringing women to the bed.

When guys are hurt they have no idea of how to handle it. Women are stronger creatures in that aspect. We take all the bullshit these guys throw at us until we get tired of it. If we were to dish out to them what they dish out to us, they could never take it. Their feelings get hurt and then they don't want to show real emotion, so they turn their feelings of hurt into anger and physical aggression. Pay attention the next time that a man you know, whether it be your friend, brother cousin, uncle godbrother, whatever…..pay attention to how they deal with emotion and heartbreak in comparison to any woman you know. Put that information into your mental rolodex because one day you are going to need to use it.

Eric and I continued to have or ups and downs. We used beans a lot so that helped to keep us at ease with each other. Our lifestyle of partying continued. We met this young lady who was actually a cousin to our neighbor at the time. She was cool. Didn't know her that well, but we chilled and smoked together. She had been coming by to see her cousin frequently and for a brief moment she even lived next door because she was trying to get her life together. Like I said, she was cool, but definitely a loner. She not only smoked but she also hit the Yoda as well. She would joke around with us sometimes. One day she was clowning around with Eric while we were smoking with her. Eric said, "Girl, you know you want me," in a laughing manner. She said, "No actually I want your wife," and we all laughed. I thought nothing of it. Plus I had seen her with guys coming by the house to see her.

I frequented our neighbor's house because there were females there. My neighbor usually had a roommate that was female as well; so I wasn't always up in Eric's face because he got on my nerves sometimes. Don't get me wrong, I love Eric, but he is a guy and sometimes he just doesn't understand what I'm talking about and he cannot relate to me in many ways. Going to hang out with my neighbor was a way to have girl time, which is what was needed. Eric had guy time with his friends too. Although, he didn't have many friends, he spent time with the few that he had. So as it is known, my life consists of working and partying. Every now and then I will volunteer or do a march to sponsor a nonprofit, but for the most part I want to enjoy life and partying was my way to enjoy life. Plus, I am a very sexual person. That is why keeping our sex life spicy is very important. I get bored easily and I need to feel wanted. I make him feel wanted and I expect the same in return.

One night, while chilling next door with my neighbor's cousin, she just out of the blue said, "Yo, I really want to eat your pussy. Can I do that?" I had a baffled look on my face, like what? I said, "Come again?" she replied, "Exactly, I want to make you come, will you let me lick your pussy?" Damn I did hear her correctly. I thought I was hearing things. I thought to myself, *where is this coming from*. She said, "Come on I been paying attention to you since I moved in over here. I'm sure Eric doesn't mind." Speaking of Eric, let me run this home real quick so we don't have any problems. I told her that I would be right back. I went next door to my house and had a quick conversation with my husband who was very tickled with the entire situation. He was fine with it, of course.

I went back and told her to come over to my house. While we were in the bed, we rolled up a blunt and the three of us smoked together. She didn't even wait for the blunt to end; she got in front of me, pulled off my panties and just went to work. Damn she knew what she was doing too. Straight to business. Forget all that foreplay, she wanted pussy. At that moment, I was happy to give her what she wanted because she knew exactly what she was doing. She was flipping her tongue and working her way around my clit better than most that I have had. She is much better than Eric, but I couldn't tell him that. His little feelings would be hurt, and he would never get over that. She was really good. I could hardly keep my composure. I did not have an orgasm often from receiving oral sex, but my goodness she had my toes curling.

Eric was lying in the bed watching all of this transpire. I told him to come to me and began giving him oral while she did me. I could hardly get in good to give it to him because what she was doing to me was feeling so good. I was feeling like... can I keep her please? She can move in. She would stop every once in a while and take a bump and go back in. I mean she was nose deep all up in my vagina and I loved every bit of it. The three of us were getting it in so good that Eric had to relieve himself from being pleased to take a breather. Eric left the room briefly. Home girl was still giving head like she was born to do this. Like it was her life's calling to devour pussy. It got so good that the bed was bouncing up and down to the beat of her neck movements. I had never experienced anything like this before. I was making noises out of feeling good, but I was also a little tickled because this girl was out of control. Damn, where they do that at???? My goodness.

Eric came back into the room and saw the bed bouncing up and down. His face said it all. It was like a scene in a movie. He had this half smile, half astonished look on his face. He and I caught each other's eyes and smirked at each other as if to say DAYUM!!!!!!!!! By the time she was finished, I was exhausted. I knew that if I was this tired, I knew she had to be ready to pass out. When I tell you that, that was one experience I will never forget for the rest of my life. Yes she had great head skills, but she was quite entertaining, as well. I mean, you don't see this type of interaction on a regular basis. I was so tickled.

She was one of the first girls that I met that loved nothing but vagina. She didn't want any parts of a man. The females that Eric and I dealt with in the past were into girls and guys so that we all could enjoy each other, but this girl only wanted me and that was different. The females in the past were definitely attracted to me and some wanted me more than Eric, but they knew that he came with the package. This girl said no to anything having to do with Eric. That was fine with me, I didn't mind pleasing Eric, he was my man, but this entire experience was so very different. I was smiling for days after that event.

Eric and I had an eventful sex life, but that was because in the beginning we both worked hard. Eric took a few years from working, which did piss me off initially and caused me to party even more. I was the only one taking care of everyone, so I deserved to enjoy myself when it was time to turn up. Even when he wasn't working, I made sure to provide enough for our partying and he still had multiple women in his bed besides me. I felt that I was doing everything that I could to make my man happy. Even if at time, I didn't totally agree with what was going on. One day, my friend Claudia asked me if I allow what goes on in our bedroom because that is what Eric likes. I didn't answer her immediately because it did make me think about that. At the time, I lied to her and said no. I told her it was because I liked it too. I did like to have women attracted to me, but I think the part that was annoying and almost unbearable to me was how Eric would show his attraction towards other women and talk about what he would do if he had the chance with this one or that one.

It wasn't the fact that we were living what some people wish they could, I liked that part. I liked how it felt. The first time a female rubbed up against me naked with boobs on my back, I realized what it was that men liked about women. Women were soft and supple and smell good and have this flirty charm. Men can be so dumb and many of them make me question their mere existence. I truly feel as if some guys were put on this earth just to provide penis. I am not saying that all men are idiots, but even the smartest, well kept, charming man has his moments that make a woman question why they even gave that man the time of day.

Now I am not saying that I am full on lesbian, because I enjoy and prefer penis in my life; however, it's always nice to have a bonus and having a female to do those things that your man may not be great at is all the more reason to invite her along for the ride. This is the true meaning of having a good time. So it wasn't the fact that we had a sex life that was unlike most, it was the way that he handled himself, the relationship and moving forward that made me question if I was content in our arrangement.

A few years back, Eric and I met a young lady that frequented the home downstairs from us. We all met at the same time and she was cool, but very young. We all formed a friendship pretty quickly. Although she did not seem like the type that would indulge us in our extracurricular activities, she was very funny, and we had some things in common, and most of all, she smoked weed also as much as we did. She told me that she noticed us because she would see us coming home from work with our daughter. Eric and I have a daughter who is very beautiful and whose eyes are a gorgeous greenish and hazel-like color.

The girl's name was Shica. She was always at the home downstairs from us, visiting her god brother. One day Shica and her godbrother caught me outside when I was arriving home from work with my daughter in tow. She introduced herself to me as I was headed to my apartment. I said hi and she expressed that she just wanted to meet the parents of this beautiful little girl. At first, I looked at her sideways, because I am very protective of my daughter. I think she realized that I was not comfortable with her initial introduction, so she elaborated. That is when she said that she had been seeing us when she would be visiting downstairs and I was a little more relieved. I was thinking she was a stalker or something. While we stood outside talking, my husband pulled into the parking lot and got out of the car looking at me like who are you talking to. We made eye contact as he walked up. I told him who she was and introduced them. By this time, her god brother had come outside and the four of us stood out there talking for a short moment before going inside. And that was that. We would see either of them or both of them in passing and say hello. I wasn't really trying to make any new friends.

Eric and I went out one night to a party at a spot where there would be a lot of young folks of color hanging out. There was good music and we had some drinks. We actually met up with some of our friends there, as well. These were friends that we have known for years, so we always had good time with them. Some of these friends have been around for the duration of our marriage; so it is like they have been on this journey with us. After having a great time at the club, we decided to head home because we were ready to smoke a blunt and it was already late. Some of our friends were actually headed to our house also because we had one of those homes where people were comfortable to be themselves.

Open Marriage

As we were walking out to our car we noticed these two people walking towards us that looked very familiar. As they walked further in our direction, I said to Eric, "Baby, aren't those the two that we met at the apartment the other day?" Eric said, "Sure is. Now y'all know it's past your bedtime, what ya doing out here?" talking to Shica and her godbrother. Shica responded, "Apparently, the same thing y'all doing out here." We all laughed for a moment. "Actually, we were just leaving," I said. Eric followed up with, "You can feel free to stop by, when y'all leave, and we will still be up." I looked at him with the look. The look you give someone when you want them to shut up. Then I smiled as I said, "Y'all have a good night." We parted ways and Eric and I headed home to meet our friends who had already pulled out of the parking lot. Not shortly after leaving, my cell phone began to ring. Our friends had arrived at our house and we were not there yet. I let them know that we would be there in a minute because we had to stop at the store for blunts and something to drink. As we were driving, Eric asked me how I felt about the downstairs neighbor and Shica. I told him that I thought they were alright. The girl was funny, and I liked to laugh.

As time went on, we all became closer. They would frequent our house since they were downstairs. Although Shica did not live downstairs, she was over there all of the time. After that, we started hanging out more often. It became to be a good thing because she was someone that I could go out with when I wanted some free time from Eric. Shica started to become a regular staple in our household. She would help us with our daughter when we needed a sitter or someone to do her hair. I was great at many things, but doing hair was not one of them. I always knew that I would have to pay someone to do my hair and when I became pregnant with a girl, all of my friends and family asked me who was going to do her hair. I would say, "I have no idea," laughing. I knew that I would have to budget in keeping my daughter's hair done.

We met her when our daughter was about two years old, so the fact that she built up trust with me was good. I could trust that she would not do anything to harm my child and that was the main issue at first. Shica would offer to take our daughter on play dates with other little kids so that Eric and I could have some time to ourselves. Eric even gave her a key to our house, in case she needed to get in when we weren't there. Of course, he didn't inform me of this, until I noticed she was in our house before we arrived home one day, and I absolutely had questions. I did not conduct an interrogation, but I did ask how she got inside. She told me that Eric gave her a key.

You know, Eric and I had a very intense conversation after that. First and foremost, you don't just offer another female a key to our home without your wife not only being informed, but a discussion was supposed to be had before that gesture was performed. I was very pissed at Eric. He did not see it as a problem because we were cool with her. I had to explain to him that cool or uncool, you don't just pass out the key to your home all willy nilly. We did not have a key to her house. I didn't even know where she lived. This gave me concerns with Eric's decision-making ability at this point. I looked at him sideways because he is not making smart decisions. I am feeling like, "Who are you?" towards him right now. We finished our very heated discussion. I decided not to take the key back from her because that would have been quite tacky in trying to undo what Eric had already done. This goes back to what I was saying about guys being idiots sometimes. I just don't understand what goes on inside his head.

Time passed by and things calmed down with Eric and me. It was a rough time for a short while because I stopped speaking to Eric for a few days. He had to get flowers and take me on a nice date to get me to talk to him because that key situation had me livid, but anyway we were now past it and moving forward. Some time had passed, and we became even closer to Shica and a couple of her friends. One of her friends that we started to get close to was a young lady named Lisa. Now remember, these females were much younger than Eric and I. Lisa would hang out at our house too and one night she rolled with Eric and me and we all just hung out. Lisa began to tell us her situation and she was not in a good place. She was living in an apartment, but her roommate had left her high and dry and she was 3 months behind in her rent. With the job that she had she was only working part time and could never make 3 months' rent in time with her income. While I felt bad for her, I said to myself that we could not let her stay with us. When we lived in central Florida together we had the house that we called Haven of Hope. I believed both Eric and I were lost souls trying to find our way. That is what kept us together. We were always trying to help someone and when we were in central Florida, we allowed a lot of people to sleep on our couch. I swear every other month we had a stranger sleeping on our couch. That is how I know that God has been watching over my life since I was a child because I have been in some possibly dangerous situations and I was never harmed.

We had good hearts, but we weren't thinking our decisions through because we were so young and felt that all people were good… some just needed more help than others. If it wasn't someone that I worked with, it was someone that he worked with and our roommate at the time had the same problem. We offered our couch to anyone that we knew that did not have a place to lay their head. We had good intentions but looking in hindsight realizing that things could have really turned out bad. After we got married, I told Eric that I did not want to allow anyone to live with us in that way. Especially once we parted ways with roommates and started living together as a couple. We continued to chill and we all collectively tried to come up with ideas to help her out in her situation. Lisa was a young female and her body was very petite. I knew Eric was attracted to her even though she was very young.

I swear I could read his thoughts. As I said to myself, *no she is not living here*, I could see his thought process happening, and I knew he was going to ask me. Remember, at this time, I am the only person in our household working. I am already taking care of Eric and our child. I do not need another mouth to feed that isn't my child. So the night ended, and the sun was starting to come up. Eventually, Lisa left, and it was just Eric and me. We began to talk about Lisa and her situation. I really felt bad for her. I have been blessed enough to never have been in a situation where I didn't know where I was going to live. It was definitely a very tense situation because I knew exactly what he was going to ask me. I continued to think of different ways to help but I wasn't coming up with anything. Finally the moment that I was dreading came. Eric asked me if Lisa could stay with us. I looked at him and I said no and I knew you were going to ask me that, but I told you that I didn't want anybody else to live with us since we left Central Florida; and now that we have a child we don't need anybody living in our house. Eric responded, "Why can't we help this poor girl out?" In response, "She is not our responsibility!"

Now don't get me wrong, I definitely felt bad for her and wanted her to find somewhere to live; but with us having a child I didn't feel it was safe to allow anybody else to move in with us. But with this person being so young and me having a daughter myself, I didn't want them on the streets trying to find someplace to live and somewhere to lay her head. But I'm being who I am… I still didn't want this person living in the house, so I told Eric no. He was visibly upset and did not speak to me for a while after that, which I was fine with. Days are gone by and we still had a talk over the situation; he continued to try to persuade me to change my mind, but I stood my ground. After three days of begging and pleading with me, Eric still didn't give up. He asked, "What would it take for you to allow this child to stay here just until she finds another place or gets her situation together?" I said "honestly, I haven't thought about it because that is not an option in my opinion." Eric said, "I promise, I will be on my best behavior and I will make sure that she is not a burden around here. You will have dinner ready when you get home from work and the house will be clean and I will personally help her to find a job." In response I said, "Eric you haven't even found a job for yourself. How are you going to find her a job? And stop making promises that you aren't going to keep. You have made several promises to me that you have broken. You said you would stop smoking and doing ecstasy when I got pregnant with our child, but you didn't, and you lied to me about it. I stopped smoking and indulging in extracurricular activities. You never did and then lied to me about it when I knew you were high. So don't tell me what you are going to do, because you are not."

I guess he got offended because his Face started turning red, "What are you talking about?" Eric responded. "I am talking about all of the things you said you would do and lied about!" "You don't know what you are talking about. I didn't roll when you were pregnant."

"Eric you rolled several times, when I was pregnant. I even asked you one day and finally confessed after I kept calling you out about it. I know what the signs are. And then you lied about it until I pointed out facts that you could not deny, so please stop pretending that you don't know what I am talking about." Eric stopped arguing with me. He must have started thinking about the things that he was saying and realizing that I was right about the situation. A few days had passed, and Lisa was at our house again. This time she came by to let us know that she had finally gotten evicted. We sat and talked, and Eric and I tried to come up with ideas to help her.

After about an hour, Eric asked if he could talk to me in the room. I knew where this conversation was going. I went into the room with Eric and he began again to ask the same question that caused us to have an argument a few days prior. I said, "Eric, I told you I do not want someone else living with us." Eric responded, "What about Paul, you let him stay here." I replied, "Yes, I was fine with Paul staying here because it was for two weeks while his place was being prepared for him to move in. Lisa has nowhere to go and that means she will be here indefinitely, and I don't have time for that. And I asked you if Paul could stay here before I told him anything." Eric responded, "Okay, how about we let her stay here, but let her know that she has to get her things in order to be moving out as soon as possible." I said, "how about no." I felt bad for Lisa and I did want to offer her the couch until she got on her feet, but I knew my husband was attracted to her and I would be setting myself up. I knew it was my insecurities that kept me from wanting to help Lisa, but she was much younger with a nice petite frame and

I could tell that he noticed. I did want to help her, but not for the sake of losing my man to some bull.

The more and more I thought about it, the more I softened up. I knew that God would bless me for helping others and this situation was no different. I knew that Lisa has no family and real close friends in this city that she can call on for help because she was from Chicago. After a lot of thought and praying, I decided that I could not allow the girl to sleep in the streets. I told Eric that she could stay, and I put down some ground rules. We would not be having sexual relations with her and he needed to help her find a job. Eric smiled and said, "Doesn't it feel good to help someone in need? I said, "Don't make me regret this decision," as I gave him a side eye.

We walked out of the room and went over to Lisa who was sitting on the couch in the living room. I began talking, "Ok Lisa, this is what we are going to do. You can stay here for a very short time. Enough time for you to get a job and get your own place. Eric is going to be working with you to help you find a job. Since both of you are looking for work, you can help each other find jobs and you can help with doing the little one's hair and helping out around the house." Lisa hugged me and said, "Thank you." the three of us continued to talk about expectations and so forth and so on. I was still a little concerned because this husband of mine was too overjoyed. Anyway, I had done a good thing, so I felt good. The next day we went to Lisa's old place and got the rest of her things that she asked a neighbor to hold for her. We then went back to the house to help Lisa organize her stuff in a corner of the living room and get her situated. Now while all of this has transpired, we never mentioned to Shica that her friend was moving in with us temporarily. I didn't think anything of it.

A little time had passed by and another weekend was now upon us. Shica and her godbrother came by to hang out as they usually did on a Friday. When she walked in the house, she was in a joking mood and we loved to laugh with each other. For example, on the night that Shica had come by after the club, we all had a ball. One of our friends who was at our house was really high on something because his jaw just kept moving around and around in circles. Shica looked at me and said, "What is wrong with him?" Her godbrother chimed in. "Yes he is obviously on something other than weed," he said, while laughing. I told them that the friend tells his girlfriend that it's from alcohol. The godbrother was like, "That ain't from just alcohol, he is on something," So I let them know that he was rolling, plus I think he had hit the Yoda, which caused his jaw to move uncontrollably. Shica laughingly said, "It looks like he can chew through a bag of quarters the way that his mouth is moving." We all fell out laughing. Shica had a great sense of humor which caused me to like having her around. Especially when Eric and I had issues, she helped to break the tension in the room.

It was Friday night and she came by with her godbrother and we all smoked and chilled at the house. Lisa was actually out somewhere, so she wasn't at the house at the moment. Her stuff was in the corner of the living room. After being there for a while, she asked, "Whose stuff is in the corner?" I told her to ask Eric. Shica looked at Eric and asked the question again. Eric responded, "That's Lisa's stuff, she got evicted." She got upset, Why y'all letting her stay here? Y'all are my friends, she needs to figure her own situation out!" I said, "Shica, I couldn't let the girl sleep out on the street and this is only temporary. Plus, I thought she was your friend, what happened?' She proceeds to tell me how she and Lisa had a disagreement and were not on good terms with each other. "Shica, no worries, she won't be here long. And she really needed someone to step in and help her get it together." Now that that was over with we could all go back to what we were doing. The conversation was over.

It had been a few weeks since Lisa moved in. So far, so good. She was making sure that my daughter's hair was laid which was very helpful. As I previously mentioned, doing hair was never my specialty. Now, my sister loves to do hair. If she were here, I would never have hair issues for myself or my child, but I digress. Lisa was not a terrible addition to the house, but she needed to find her a job. I was starting to re-think this decision because when I look at the bigger picture, I am the only one leaving to go to work every day, while I leave my husband alone with Lisa. My insecurities started to build again, but I allowed her to stay because she had not done anything to cause concern. When it came to partying on the weekend this was another mouth drinking the liquor, smoking the blunt and wanting ecstasy. I only gave her liquor and weed. If she wanted to roll she was going to have to support her own habit... *I'm just saying.*

We did our usual on a weekend, got some party favors and relaxed. This time, it was just Eric, Lisa and me listening to music and chilling. One of my favorite songs came on and I got up and started singing. "Like a g6, like a g6 ..." I liked to dance to this tune, so I started singing and dancing. Just having a good time. Lisa got up and started dancing with me. She started dancing on me very provocatively, I said, "Hold up now" don't get too close. As I laughed. We kept dancing and the song went off. I told her, "No offense, but that is not going to happen. It's too close for comfort. I hope you understand." She said, "Girl I was just dancing with you, that's all." I said ok. I started to feel my bean, so I became touchy feely with Eric. He was sitting next to me on the couch. It's a shame how predictable he was, I swear. After we had been hanging out for a while, we started to kiss a little bit and he asked Lisa to sit next to him. I looked at him and said, "Alright, don't make me have to hurt you." He said, better yet, Lisa, you stay where you are at." As he laughed. I reminded Eric of what the stipulations were for Lisa staying at our house.

Later on that night, we ran out of cigarettes and when we were rolling, menthol cigarettes were a necessity. I asked Eric to go get cigarettes and he was very hesitant. I decided to go get them myself because he was acting funny. It's all good, I am a big girl, I can go to the store by myself. "Lisa, c'mon ride with me to the corner store." Lisa replied, 'Naw, I'm good, it's cold out there." "Alright fine, I will go by myself." I looked at Eric and gave him a piercing eye stare. As if to say, you better be good. I left and went to the store. I walked into the gas station, "Hi can I get Newport shorts in a box please?" The cashier handed me the cigarettes and I paid with my card and was out.

While headed back to the house, I noticed my neighbor outside of the building. She and I sat outside and talked for a while. She was updating me on what's been going on in her life and vice versa. After we talked for a while I went inside. I was almost expecting to walk in on something, but I didn't. Both Lisa and Eric were in the same spot where I left them. That was a good thing. I still had to keep this situation on my radar. A couple of months go by and everything is going well. The only downfall to having Lisa staying with us is that we never had any leftovers while she lived in the house. She was small, but she could sure eat. Everything remained in good status to my knowledge. The weekend was coming up, so I decided to stop by the liquor store to pick up a bottle of Patron and some fresh limes. I also stopped by homeboy's to get some party favors because that is simply what we did when the weekend came around.

I pulled into the parking lot and got out of the car. While getting the bags out of the car, I had to place them strategically so all of the weight would be on one side because I had groceries and my purse and lunch box from work. Talk about a bag lady. I fumbled with the keys a bit to make sure not to drop them, since I had a million and one bags in my arms. Finally, I got the keys that I needed to open the door. I got inside and went directly to the kitchen. I placed everything down on the kitchen counter. I noticed that no one was home, which was strange because we only had one car. I wondered where they could be and then I thought, *oh well, they will be back.* I went and closed the front door and locked it. I began to put the food and drinks away and put the Patron in the freezer so it can be chilled. I headed to my room because as anyone knows, you must go to the bathroom upon entering your home, it's an unspoken rule that your body makes up early in life.

As I entered our room which was the master with a bathroom inside, I noticed Eric in the bed with his face in the sheets, or at least that is how it appeared at first. As I got closer, I saw Lisa in my bed with her legs spread eagle and Eric nose deep in her pussy. Once I realized what I was seeing with my own eyes, I tiptoed backwards so they wouldn't notice that I had even walked in. I'm so glad my boss asked me if wanted to leave early since I had worked overtime that week. I was supposed to leave work early so that I can catch these two. I went into the kitchen to collect my thoughts and figure out my next move. I was pacing back and forth and finally I grabbed a big butcher knife out of the knife holder and headed straight for the room. I busted the room door open with knife in tow. "Oh, ok, so this is how you are gonna play me?? Both of you backstabbing bastards," I yelled, while I swung the knife at them. Both of them screaming, "Wait, no I'm sorry, it's not what you think, we didn't mean to hurt you….." I wasn't hearing any of the lies that either of them was saying. I saw red; all I could see was them running away while I swung a big knife at them. I swung at Eric's penis, "Since you don't know how to use your little thing the right way how about I help you with that.

They both ran out of the bedroom into the living room. "What the hell were you thinking? I told you Eric, that we were not going down that road, but you went anyway. And Lisa you fucking slut, get the hell out of my home. I take care of you, stupid. I am the one that buys the food you have been eating and I pay the rent here where you are laying your head and you want to throw your tired ass pussy at my husband… and Eric… you are stupid. You really fucked up. I am the best thing that you will ever come across. Nobody is going to take your bullshit! Fuck this. Get out… both of you!!!! Get out!!!"

I went over to the corner where Lisa's stuff was and began tossing it outside over the banister. "Take all of your shit with you." Eric stood there looking at me as if he didn't know what to do. I said to him, "Go ahead and go with your new boo because we are done." I backed both of them out of the house completely naked before I started tossing her stuff outside. After I finished with her items I locked the front door and went into the kitchen and poured a shot of Patron. Eric began knocking on the door. "Baby, open the door, please don't leave me out here without any clothes, baby please, open up." I opened the door and tossed a heapful of Eric's clothes at him and shut the door and locked it. I went back to the kitchen and I put the knife down on the counter and poured another shot of Patron.

I should have stabbed one of their asses, can't believe these mf's just tried me. I gave him everything that a man could want. He had a fine pretty wife with morals and ethics and does not have a problem with working and being career-oriented and allowed threesomes and more than that sometimes. This dude was living the life and he still wasn't happy… he still had to go mess with this chick. And she's stupid because I was trying to help her dumb ass. Now they can both go find somewhere to stay together because they ain't coming back in here. I'm so pissed. I knew better. What the hell was I thinking? I am trying to be a good Christian woman and open my home up to a stranger out of the kindness of my heart. Never again, lesson learned. I'm done with trying to make this work.

I changed the way that I do things to make him happy. I have dealt with him not treating me like the queen that I am because I love him. Fuck love it don't live here anymore. I stood in the kitchen with the bottle of Patron as I poured shot after shot until my heartbeat began to slow down. I grabbed the limes, the bottle of Patron, rolled a blunt and sat on the couch trying to calm down. As I puffed on the blunt I took another shot of Patron. Now it is quiet, and I have time to think. That is absolutely the last thing that anyone in trouble wants to hear; that his woman has had time to think out a strategy of revenge.

See I am not the person for all that drama. I don't need extra in my life; there is enough to my life without adding extra drama. I acted out of anger and they are lucky I didn't land that knife on one of them. It took a while for me to loosen up, but after all those shots of Patron I was finally starting to get a little tipsy. That night seemed so long. I cried, I laughed, I talked to myself I pictured cussing them out while no one was there with me. It was like a scene from a movie. Someone would have really thought that I was diagnosed with a mental illness after seeing my episode that night. I fell asleep on the couch in tears with the bottle next to me.

I woke up the next morning, trying to figure out what had happened the night before and if it was real or if I was dreaming. I saw the bottle of Patron and half-smoked blunt and realized that it was not a dream. I went to find my phone in the room. I hadn't even checked my phone since I left work the day before. I looked at the notifications, 25 missed calls. Most of the missed calls were from Eric and I did not pay attention to the rest. My voicemail was full also. On my voicemail, "Baby, I'm sorry, please let me back in the house. It's not what you think, I can explain," the typical lines that someone-who -knows-they-did-wrong response.

It was now Saturday and I refused to answer the phone or door for Eric. I had to figure out what I wanted to do. Did I want to stay in this relationship, did I want to leave, what do you want to do girl? is what I kept asking myself, as I didn't know what I wanted. It's a good thing my daughter was away at a friend's house spending the weekend. This was too much drama for her to see. Saturday, I sulked and cried and blamed myself for putting up with his shit for so long. I did grow to love him and envision the rest of my life with him. Now what? I always wanted to be married so that I could have someone that I had sex with regularly and I wouldn't be living in sin. I liked sex and I liked feeling wanted and being touched and felt up by someone that is doing those things with the right intentions. I didn't want to be alone. All of these thoughts were going through my head. I spent most of Saturday on the couch, crying like a baby.

Sunday morning, it had been 2 days since I kicked Eric and Lisa out of our home. The audacity of the two of them. I was hurt and pissed all at the same time. How could he do this after I made it clear that it would be a problem if she moved in. He begged me for this. He probably had this planned all along, thinking he could persuade me to go along with that bullshit too. How stupid is he? Probably as stupid as I am for putting up with this bull that is him. And that heifer knows that she cannot step foot back into this house. I should have kicked her ass, or at least cut her up with that knife. I just don't have time for fighting. First of all, I am not fighting over a dude; and secondly, I am too pretty for all of that. And she must be the dumbest of them all. She had a place to stay and lay her head… and she effed that up.

Oh well, I did what I could to help her dumb ass. God will bless me. He knows my heart and knows that my intentions are good. I have not been a perfect person in my life; but I have continued to work on being a better productive person to society, my family and myself. I just want the best for my child, myself and my family. How was I going to go on now as a single parent with my daughter,? I have no idea how I should move forward. I got up off the couch and walked around the house. I was looking for Eric's favorite thing. What is it that Eric loves in here? Then a light bulb went off in my head. It was like "Ding!" I headed for the television in the living room. Eric is in love with his video games. He had a play station 1, 2 & 3; plus, he had vintage games like Nintendo and Sega genesis. Underneath the TV stand was all of his game paraphernalia and anything else that he used to play video games. I stood there with a big smile on my face. I walked over to the garbage in the kitchen and grabbed a big box that was on the floor ready to be thrown out. I took the box and placed all of his game consoles, games, etc. and placed all of them in the box. First, I took every video game and DVD and stepped on them after throwing them to the ground. I stomped on them several times to make sure that they were good and crushed. Then I cut all of the wires to the wires that connected the controllers to the consoles and to the television. I took the game consoles and smashed them to the ground one by one, getting joy out of each one that was destroyed, more and more. After I cut up the wires and destroyed every item in the box, I took it outside and put it on the ground behind the back tire of the car. I got into the car and backed the car up over the box over and over and over and over again. I continued that until I was satisfied with my intent to destroy him. Once I was happy with the items being destroyed, I left the box in the parking lot, went upstairs and grabbed some of Eric's clothes and all of the items within reach that I knew that he adored and loved, and took it outside to put in the box with the destroyed items in the parking lot. I then walked upstairs and entered the apartment and rolled up a nice fat ass spliff. I grabbed the lighter fluid, the lighter and the spliff and went back to the box outside on the ground. I proceeded to light the blunt, pour lighter fluid in the box on top of his adorned items and lit that bitch!!!! I sat on the trunk of my car watched all of Eric's precious memories go up in flames. I enjoyed sitting outside, watching his stuff burn. There were some paper items so that helped to keep the fire going.

I wanted his heart to break the way that my heart was broken. I wanted to see him cry and get emotional the way that I have been these last few days. I have done everything for this man. I have allowed things in this relationship that other women would not accept. I have taken care of our entire family while he sat his ass at home claiming to be looking for a job. I shared everything that I had with him. When my family would do things for me or give me things, I always made sure that he was included. I downplayed my feelings, thoughts and reactions to appease him. I allowed him to take my crown. I really became a puppet for this dude. He never deserved me, but I kept on being persistent. His mother and his sister never liked me because I was the woman in his life, and they can't stand it. They can have him now. I wanted him, but maybe he is not what God wants for me. Then I had an epiphany. It was at this moment that I realized that I had been going about this relationship stuff all wrong.

I picked Eric because I wanted someone that was laid back and mild-mannered. I didn't feel threatened with him. I didn't feel like he was a player or someone that chased skirts, like Shawn. Shawn was a hoe and that has kept me from taking him seriously in regard to a relationship, but his sex was very good. I was never head over heels for Eric when we started dating, but I felt that I could learn to love him. I chose him. God didn't choose him for me. Yes, Eric was attractive and had good qualities, but we didn't have an instant connection or love at first sight feelings when we met. I just thought that he was cute and easy to deal with and he had some education under his belt. After I graduated from college, I stayed in the city because people were familiar to me. I was terrified of leaving my college town without a significant other that I would eventually marry. I was also afraid to step out into the world of dating and meeting strangers because I feared that if I didn't marry someone that I met in college, then I was not going to get married. I did not trust God to send me the man that he has picked specifically for me.

This entire situation has totally opened my eyes to a different way of looking at the world. I was absolutely still hurt, but I was still unclear on what to do moving forward. At this point, I am broken. My heart is broken, my trust is broken, and my spirit is broken.

1 Corinthians 13:4-8 says:

***4** Love is patient, love is kind. It does not envy, it does not boast, it is not proud.*

***5** It does not dishonor others, it is not self-seeking, it is not easily angered, it keeps no record of wrongs.*

6 Love does not delight in evil but rejoices with the truth.

7 It always protects, always trusts, always hopes, always perseveres.

8 Love never fails.

With that being said, I felt at that moment that I was not in a loving relationship and that if he truly loves me he would show me. Otherwise, we don't need to be together. I need time to figure out what I want and what God wants for me. My time will be focused on prayer and fasting because it is obvious that I am not currently walking in the way that I should, and I need help.

Oh Lord, Please help me!

ABOUT THE AUTHOR

Tiffany McGee was born Tiffany Covington in Miami, FL to a loving mother and father who were very young parents.. Tiffany's mother moved on to marry and establish a family which brought about a younger sister when Tiffany was a toddler.

Tiffany was raised with God as her foundation and eventually graduated from high school and went away to college at Florida State University where she received her Bachelor of Science in Family and Child Science.

Tiffany moved around Florida over the years. During that time she married and had a child. After 13 years of marriage, they divorced. She settled back at home in South Florida where she currently resides. She loves her family and spends time with them as much as possible.

As a single mom and career woman, Tiffany has earned her Master's degree in Human Resource Management and continues to work on her writing. **Open Marriage** is Tiffany McGee's first published novel.

CPSIA information can be obtained
at www.ICGtesting.com
Printed in the USA
JSHW032233190622
27231JS00003B/17